MORE SHAPES

THAN ONE

Books by Fred Chappell

NOVELS

It Is Time, Lord
The Inkling
Dagon
The Gaudy Place
I Am One of You Forever
Brighten the Corner Where You Are

SHORT STORIES

Moments of Light

POETRY

The World Between the Eyes
River
The Man Twice Married to Fire
Bloodfire
Awakening to Music
Wind Mountain
Earthsleep
Driftlake: A Lieder Cycle
Midquest
Castle Tzingal
Source
First and Last Words

ANTHOLOGIES

The Fred Chappell Reader

Fred Chappell

MORE SHAPES

THAN ONE

St. Martin's Press • New York

"Linnaeus Forgets" first appeared in *American Review 26*; then in *Florist's Review* (May 11, 1978) and in *The Fred Chappell Reader* (St. Martin's Press, 1987).

"Ladies from Lapland," *The Akros Review* (Fall 1981).

"The Snow That Is Nothing in the Triangle," *Georgia Review* (Winter 1981) and in *Necessary Fictions* (The University of Georgia Press, 1986).

"Barcarole," *The Chattahoochee Review* (Spring 1984).

"Weird Tales," *The Texas Review* (Summer 1984) and in *The Year's Best Horror Stories, Series XIII* (DAW Books, 1985).

"The Adder," *Deathrealm* (#9, 1989) and in *The Year's Best Fantasy and Horror, Third Annual Collection* (St. Martin's Press, 1989).

"Ember," *Weird Tales* (Fall 1990).

"Duet," *Appalachian Heritage* (Spring 1975) and in *The Uneven Ground* (Kentucke Imprints, 1985).

"Miss Prue," *Cold Mountain Review* (Spring 1981).

"Mankind Journeys Through Forests of Symbols," *Madison Review* (Winter 1988), and in *The Sewanee Review* (Summer 1991).

"After Revelation," *Denver Quarterly* (Fall 1985).

Design by Dawn Niles

Library of Congress Cataloging-in-Publication Data

Chappell, Fred.
    More shapes than one / Fred Chappell.
        p.   cm.
    ISBN 0-312-06418-7
    I. Title.
    PS3553.H298M64 1991
    813'.54—dc20   91-20551
                                                         CIP

First Edition: September 1991

10 9 8 7 6 5 4 3 2 1

for Helene Nicholls

CONTENTS

Linnaeus Forgets   1
Ladies from Lapland   19
The Snow That Is Nothing in the
                        Triangle   31
Barcarole   43
Weird Tales   58
The Somewhere Doors   71
The Adder   98
Ember   122
Duet   133
Miss Prue   150
Mankind Journeys Through Forests of
                        Symbols   155
Alma   169
After Revelation   186

For who knows not that Truth is strong, next to the Almighty. She needs no policies, nor stratagems nor licensings to make her victorious—those are the shifts and defenses that error uses against her power . . . .

Yet is it not impossible that she may have more shapes than one.

—MILTON, *Areopagitica*

LINNAEUS FORGETS

 The year 1758 was a comparatively happy one in the life of Carl Linnaeus. For although his second son, Johannes, had died the year before at the age of three, in that same year his daughter Sophia, the last child he was to have, was born. And in 1758 he purchased three small bordering estates in the country near Uppsala and on one of these, Hammarby, he established a retreat, to which he thereafter retired during the summer months, away from the town and its deadly fever. He was content in his family, his wife and five children living; and having recently been made a Knight of the Polar Star, he now received certain intelligence that at the opportune hour he would be ennobled by King Adolph Fredrik.

The landscape about Hammarby was pleasant and interesting, though of course Linnaeus long ago had observed and classified every botanical specimen this region had to offer. Even so, he went almost daily on long walks into the countryside, usually accompanied by students. The students could not deny themselves his presence even during vacation periods; they were attracted to him as hummingbirds to trumpet vines by his geniality and humor and by his encyclopedic knowledge of every plant springing from the earth.

And he was happy, too, in overseeing the renovations of the buildings in Hammarby and the construction of the new orangery, in which he hoped to bring to fruition certain exotic plants that had never before flowered on Swedish soil. Linnaeus had become at last a famous man, a world figure in the same fashion that Samuel Johnson and Voltaire and Albrecht von Haller were world figures, and every post brought him sheaves of adulatory verse and requests for permission to dedicate books to him and inquiries about the details of his system of sexual classification and plant specimens of every sort. Most of the specimens were flowers quite commonly known, but dried and pressed and sent to him by young ladies who sometimes hoped that they had discovered a new species, or who hoped merely to secure a token of the man's notice, an autograph letter. But he also received botanical samples from persons with quite reputable knowledge, from scientists persuaded that they had discovered some anomaly or exception that might cause him to think over again some part of his method. (For the ghost of Siegesbeck was even yet not completely laid.) Occasionally other specimens arrived that were indeed unfamiliar to him. These came from scientists and missionaries traveling in remote parts of the world, or the plants were sent by knowledgeable ship captains or now and then by some common sailor who had come to know, however vaguely and confusedly, something of Linnaeus's reputation.

His renown had come to him so belatedly and so tendentiously that the great botanist took a child's delight in all this attention. He read all the verses and all the letters and often would answer his unknown correspondents pretty much in their own manner; letters still remain to us in

which he addressed one or another of his admirers in a
silly and exaggerated prose style, admiring especially the
charms of these young ladies on whom he had never set
eyes. Sweden was in those days regarded as a backward
country, having only a few warriors and enlightened des-
pots to offer as important cultural figures, and part of Linnaeus's pride in his own achievements evinced itself in
nationalist terms, a habit that Frenchmen and Englishmen
found endearing.

On June 12, 1758, a large box was delivered to Linnaeus, along with a brief letter, and both these objects were
battered from much travel. He opened first the box and
found inside it a plant in a wicker basket that had been
lined with oilskin. The plant was rooted in a black sandy
loam, now dry and crumbly, and Linnaeus immediately
watered it from a sprinkling can, though he entertained little hope of saving—actually, resuscitating—the plant. The
plant was so wonderfully woebegone in appearance, so tat-
tered by rough handling, that the scientist could not say
immediately whether it was shrub, flower, or a tall grass.
It seemed to have collapsed in upon itself, and its tough
leaves and stems were the color of parchment and crackled
like parchment when he tried to examine them. He de-
sisted, hoping that the accompanying letter would answer
some of his questions.

The letter bore no postmark. It was signed with a Dutch
name, Gerhaert Oorts, though it was written in French. As
he read the letter, it became clear to Linnaeus that the man
who had signed it had not written it out himself but had
dictated it to someone else who had translated his words
as he spoke. The man who wrote the letter was a Dutch
sailor, a common seaman, and it was probably one of his
superior officers who had served him as amanuensis and
translator. The letter was undated and began: *"Cher maître
Charles Linné, père de la science botanique; je ne sçay si. . . ."*

"To the great Carl Linnaeus, father of botany; I know
not whether the breadth of your interests still includes a

wondering curiosity about strange plants which grow in many different parts of the world, or whether your ever-agile spirit has undertaken to possess new kingdoms of science entirely. But in case you are continuing in your botanical endeavors, I am taking liberty to send you a remarkable flower [*une fleur merveilleuse*] that my fellows and I have observed to have strange properties and characteristics. This flower grows in no great abundance on the small islands east of Guiana in the South Seas. With all worshipful respect, I am your obedient servant, Gerhaert Oorts."

Linnaeus smiled on reading this letter, amused by the odd wording, but then frowned slightly. He still had no useful information. The fact that Mynheer Oorts called the plant a flower was no guarantee that it was indeed a flower. Few people in the world were truly interested in botany, and it was not to be expected that a sailor could have leisure for even the most rudimentary study of the subject. The most he could profitably surmise was that it bore blooms, which the sailor had seen.

He looked at it again, but it was so crumpled in upon itself that he was fearful of damaging it if he undertook a hasty inspection. It was good to know that it was a tropical plant. Linnaeus lifted the basket out of the box and set the plant on the corner of a long table where the sunlight fell strongest. He noticed that the soil was already thirsty again, so he watered it liberally, still not having any expectation that his ministrations would take the least effect.

It was now quarter till two, and as he had arranged a two o'clock appointment with a troublesome student, Linnaeus hurried out of his museum—which he called "my little back room"—and went into the main house to prepare himself. His student arrived promptly but was so talkative and contentious and so involved in a number of personal problems that the rest of the afternoon was dissipated in conference with him. After this, it was time for dinner, over which Linnaeus and his family habitually sat for more than two hours, gossiping and teasing and laughing. And then there was music on the clavier in the small, rough dining room; the botanist was partial to Telemann, and sat beaming in a corner of a sofa, nodding in time to a sonata.

And so it was eight o'clock before he found opportunity to return to his little back room. He had decided to defer thorough investigation of his new specimen until the next day, preferring to examine his plants by natural sunlight rather than by lamplight. For though the undying summer twilight still held the western sky, in the museum it was gray and shadowy. But he wanted to take a final look at the plant before retiring and he needed also to draw up an account of the day's activities for his journal.

He entered the little house and lit two oil lamps. The light they shed mingled with the twilight, giving a strange orange tint to the walls and furnishings.

Linnaeus was immediately aware that changes had taken place in the plant. It was no trick of the light; the plant had acquired more color. The leaves and stems were suffused with a bright lemonish yellow, a color much more alive than the dim dun the plant had shown at two o'clock. And in the room hung a pervasive scent, unmistakable but not oppressive, which could be accounted for only by the presence of the plant. This was a pleasant perfume and full of reminiscence—but he could not remember of what the scent reminded him. So many associations crowded into his mind that he could sort none of them out; but there was nothing unhappy in these confused sensations. He wagged his head in dreamy wonder.

He looked at it more closely and saw that the plant had lost its dry parchmentlike texture, that its surfaces had become pliable and lifelike in appearance. Truly it was a remarkable specimen, with its warm perfume and marvelous recuperative powers. He began to speculate that this plant had the power of simply becoming dormant, and not dying, when deprived of proper moisture and nourishment.

He took up a bucket of well water, replenishing the watering can, and watered it again, resolving that he would give up all his other projects now until he had properly examined this stranger and classified it.

He snuffed the lamps and went out again into the vast whitish-yellow twilight. A huge full moon loomed in the east, just brushing the tree tips of a grove, and from within the grove sounded the harsh trills and staccato accents of a song sparrow and the calmly flowing recital of a thrush. The air was already cool enough that he could feel the warmth of the earth rising about his ankles. Now the botanist was entirely happy, and he felt within him the excitement he often had felt before when he came to know that he had found a new species and could enter another name and description into his grand catalogue.

He must have spent more time in his little back room than he had supposed, for when he reentered his dwelling house, all was silent and only enough lamps were burning for him to see to make his way about. Everyone had retired, even the two servants. Linnaeus reflected that his household had become accustomed to his arduous hours and took it for granted that he could look after his own desires at bedtime. He took a lamp and went quietly up the stairs to the bedroom. He dressed himself for bed and got in beside Fru Linnaea, who had gathered herself into a warm huddle on the left-hand side. As he arranged the bedclothes, she murmured some sleep-blurred words that he could not quite hear, and he stroked her shoulder and then turned on his right side to go to sleep.

But sleep did not come. Instead, bad memories rose, memories of old academic quarrels, and memories especially of the attacks upon him by Johann Siegesbeck. For when Siegesbeck first attacked his system of sexual classification in that detestable book called *Short Outline of True Botanic Wisdom*, Linnaeus had almost no reputation to speak of and Siegesbeck represented—to Sweden, at least—the authority of the academy. And what, Linnaeus asked, was the basis of this ignorant pedant's objections? Why, that his system of classifying plants was morally dissolute. In his book, Siegesbeck had asked, "Who would have thought that bluebells, lilies, and onions could be up to such immorality?" He went on for pages in this vein, not failing to point out that Sir Thomas Browne had listed the notion of the sexuality of plants as one of the vulgar errors. Finally Siegesbeck had asked—anticipating an objection Goethe would voice eighty-three years later—how such a licentious method of classification could be taught to young students without corruption of minds and morals.

Linnaeus groaned involuntarily, helpless under the force of memory.

These attacks had not let up, had cost him a position at the university, so that he was forced to support himself as a medical practitioner and for two barren years had been exiled from his botanical studies. In truth, Linnaeus never understood the nature of these attacks; they seemed foolish and irrelevant, and that is why he remembered them so bitterly. He could never understand how a man could write: "To tell you that nothing could equal the gross prurience of Linnaeus's mind is perfectly needless. A literal translation of the first principles of Linnaean botany is enough to shock female modesty. It is possible that many virtuous students might not be able to make out the similitude of *Clitoria*."

It seemed to Linnaeus that to describe his system of classification as immoral was to describe nature as immoral, and nature could not be immoral. It seemed to him that the plants inhabited a different world than the fallen world of mankind, and that they lived in a sphere of perfect freedom and ease, unvexed by momentary and perverse jealousies. Any man with eyes could see that the stamens were masculine and the pistils feminine, and that if there was only one stamen to the female part (Monandria), this approximation of the Christian European family was only charmingly coincidental. It was more likely that the female would be attended by four husbands (Tetrandria) or by five (Pentandria) or by twelve or more (Dodecandria). When he placed the poppy in the class Polyandria and described its arrangement as "Twenty males or more in the same bed with the female," he meant to say of the flower no more than God had said when He created it. How had it happened that mere literal description had caused him such unwarrantable hardship?

These thoughts and others toiled in his mind for an hour or so. When at last they subsided, Linnaeus had turned on his left side toward his wife and fallen asleep, breathing unevenly.

He rose later than was his custom. His sleep had been shaken by garish dreams that now he could not remember, and he wished he had awakened earlier. Now he got out of bed with uncertain movements and stiffly made his toilet and dressed himself. His head buzzed. He hurried downstairs as soon as he could.

It was much later than he had supposed. None of the family was about; everyone had already breakfasted and set out in pursuit of the new day. Only Nils, the elderly bachelor manservant, waited to serve him in the dining room. He informed his master that Fru Linnaea had taken all the children, except the baby asleep in the nursery, on an excursion into town. Linnaeus nodded, and wondered briefly whether the state of his accounts this quarter could support the good Fru's passion for shopping. Then he forgot about it.

It was almost nine o'clock.

He ate a large breakfast of bread and cheese and butter and fruit, together with four cups of strong black tea. After eating, he felt both refreshed and dilatory and he thought for a long moment of taking advantage of the morning and the unnaturally quiet house to read in some of the new volumes of botanical studies that had arrived during the past few weeks.

But when he remembered the new specimen awaiting him in the museum, these impulses evaporated and he left the house quickly. It was another fine day. The sky was cloudless, a mild, mild blue. Where the east grove cast its shadow on the lawn, dew still remained, and he smelled its freshness as he passed. He fumbled the latch excitedly, and then he swung the museum door open.

His swift first impression was that something had caught fire and burned, the odor in the room was so strong. It wasn't an acrid smell, a smell of destruction, but it was overpowering, and in a moment he identified it as having an organic source. He closed the door and walked to the center of the room. It was not only the heavy damp odor that attacked his senses but also a high-pitched musical chirping, or twittering, scattered on the room's laden air. And the two sensations, smell and sound, were indistinguishably mixed; here was an example of that sensory confusion of which M. Diderot had written so engagingly. At first he could not discover the source of all this sensual hurly-burly. The morning sun entered the windows to shine aslant the north wall, so that between Linnaeus and his strange new plant there fell a tall rectangular corridor of sunshine through which his gaze couldn't pierce clearly.

He stood stock-still, for what he could see of the plant beyond the light astonished him. It had opened out and grown monstrously; it was enormous, tier on tier of dark green reaching to a height of three feet or more above the table. No blooms that he could see, but differentiated levels of broad green leaves spread out in orderly fashion from bottom to top, so that the plant had the appearance of a flourishing green pyramid. And there was movement among and about the leaves, a shifting in the air all around it, and he supposed that an extensive tropical insect life had been transported into his little museum. Linnaeus smiled nervously, hardly able to contain his excitement, and stepped into the passage of sunlight.

As he advanced toward the plant, the twittering sound

grew louder. The foliage, he thought, must be rife with living creatures. He came to the edge of the table but could not see clearly yet, his sight still dazzled from stepping into and out of the swath of sunshine.

Even when his eyes grew more accustomed to shadow, he still could not make out exactly what he was looking at. There was a general confused movement about and within the plant, a continual settling and unsettling as around a beehive, but the small creatures that flitted there were so shining and iridescent, so gossamerlike, that he could fix no proper impression of them. Now, though, he heard them quite clearly, and realized that what at first had seemed a confused mélange of twittering was, in fact, an orderly progression of sounds, a music as of flutes and piccolos in polyphony.

He could account for this impression in no way but to think of it as a product of his imagination. He had become aware that his senses were not so acute as they ordinarily were; or rather, that they were acute enough, but that he was having some difficulty in interpreting what his senses told him. It occurred to him that the perfume of the plant—which now cloaked him heavily, an invisible smoke—possessed perhaps some narcotic quality. When he reached past the corner of the table to a wall shelf for a magnifying glass, he noticed that his movements were sluggish and that an odd feeling of remoteness took power over his mind.

He leaned over the plant, training his glass and trying to breathe less deeply. The creature that swam into his sight, flitting through the magnification, so startled him that he dropped the glass to the floor and began to rub his eyes and temples and forehead. He wasn't sure what he had seen—that is, he could not believe what he thought he had seen—because it was no form of insect life at all.

He retrieved the glass and looked again, moving from one area of the plant to another, like a man examining a map.

These were no insects, though many of the creatures here inhabiting were winged. They were of flesh, however diminutive they were in size. The whole animal family was represented here in miniature: horses, cows, dogs, serpents, lions and tigers and leopards, elephants, oppossums and otters. . . . All the animals Linnaeus had seen or heard of surfaced here for a moment in his horn-handled glass and then sped away on their ordinary amazing errands—and not only the animals he might have seen in the world, but the fabulous animals, too: unicorns and dragons and gryphons and basilisks and the Arabian flying serpents of which Herodotus had written.

Tears streamed on the botanist's face, and he straightened and wiped his eyes with his palm. He looked all about him in the long room, but nothing else had changed. The floor was littered with potting soil and broken and empty pots, and on the shelves were the jars of chemicals and dried leaves, and on the small round table by the window his journal lay open, with two quill pens beside it and the inkpot and his pewter snuffbox. If he had indeed become insane all in a moment, the distortion of his perceptions did not extend to the daily objects of his existence but was confined to this one strange plant.

He stepped to the little table and took two pinches of snuff, hoping that the tobacco might clear his head and that the dust in his nostrils might prevent to some degree the narcotic effect of the plant's perfume, if that was what caused the appearance of these visions. He sneezed in the sunlight and dust motes rose golden around him. He bent to his journal and dipped his pen and thought, but finally wrote nothing. What could he write down that he would believe in a week's time?

He returned to the plant, determined to subject it to the most minute examination. He decided to limit his observation to the plant itself, disregarding the fantastic animal life. With the plant, his senses would be less likely to deceive him. But his resolve melted away when once again he em-

ployed the magnifying glass. There was too much movement; the distraction was too violent.

Now he observed that there were not only miniature animals, real and fabulous, but there was also a widespread
colony, or nation, of homunculi. Here were little men and
women, perfectly formed, and—like the other animals—sometimes having wings. He felt the mingled fear
and astonishment that Mr. Swift's hapless Gulliver felt
when he first encountered the Lilliputians. But he also felt
an admiration, as he might have felt upon seeing some particularly well-fashioned example of the Swiss watch-
maker's art. To see large animals in small, with their
customary motions so accelerated, did indeed give the impression of a mechanical exhibition.

Yet there was really nothing mechanical about them, if
he put himself in their situation. They were self-determin-
ing; most of their actions had motives intelligible to him,
however exotic were the means of carrying out these motives. Here, for example, a tiny rotund man in a green jer-
kin and saffron trousers talked—sang, rather—to a tiny
slender man dressed all in brown. At the conclusion of this
recitative, the man in brown raced away and leapt onto the
back of a tiny winged camel, which bore him from this
lower level of the plant to an upper one, where he dismounted and began singing to a young lady in a bright
blue gown. Perfectly obvious that a message had been delivered. . . . Here in another place a party of men and
women mounted on unwinged great cats, lions and leopards and tigers, pursued over the otherwise-deserted broad
plain of a leaf a fearful Hydra, its nine heads snapping and
spitting. At last they impaled it to the white leaf vein with
the sharp black thorns they carried for lances and then they
set the monster afire, writhing and shrieking, and they rode
away together. A grayish waxy blister formed on the leaf
where the hydra had burned. . . . And here in another area
a formal ball was taking place, the tiny gentlemen leading
out the ladies in time to the music of an orchestra sawing
and pounding at the instruments. . . .

This plant, then, enfolded a little world, a miniature society in which the mundane and the fanciful commingled in matter-of-fact fashion but at a feverish rate of speed.

Linnaeus became aware that his legs were trembling from tiredness and that his back ached. He straightened, feeling a grateful release of muscle tension. He went round to the little table and sat, dipped his pen again, and began writing hurriedly, hardly stopping to think. He wrote until his hand almost cramped and then he flexed it several times and wrote more, covering page after page with his neat sharp script. Finally he laid the pen aside and leaned back in his chair and thought. Many different suppositions formed in his mind, but none of them made clear sense. He was still befuddled and he felt that he might be confused for years to come, that he had fallen victim to a dream or vision from which he might never recover.

In a while he felt rested and he returned again to look at the plant.

By now a whole season, or a generation or more, had passed. The plant itself was a darker green than before, its shape had changed, and even more creatures now lived within it. The mid-part of the plant had opened out into a large boxlike space thickly walled with hand-sized kidney-shaped leaves. This section formed a miniature theater or courtyard. Something was taking place here, but Linnaeus could not readily figure out what it was.

Much elaborate construction had been undertaken. The smaller leaves of the plant in this space had been clipped and arranged into a grand formal garden. There were walls and arches of greenery and greenery shaped into obelisks topped with globes, and Greek columns and balconies and level paths. Wooden statues and busts were placed at intervals within this garden, and it seemed to Linnaeus that on some of the subjects he could make out the lineaments of the great classical botanists. Here, for example, was Pliny, and there was Theophrastus. Many of the persons so honored were unfamiliar to him, but then he found on one of

the busts, occupying a position of great prominence, his
own rounded cheerful features. Could this be true? He
stared and stared, but his little glass lacked enough magnification for him to be finally certain.

Music was everywhere; chamber orchestras were sta-
tioned at various points along the outer walls of the garden
and two large orchestras were set up at either end of the
wide main path. There were a number of people calmly
walking about, twittering to one another, but there were
fewer than he had supposed at first. The air above them
was dotted with cherubs flying about playfully, and much
of the foliage was decorated with artfully hung tapestries.
There was about the scene an attitude of expectancy, of
waiting.

At this point the various orchestras began to sound in
concert and gathered the music into recognizable shape.
The sound was still thin and high-pitched, but Linnaeus
discerned in it a long reiterative fanfare, which was followed by a slow, grave processional march. All the little
people turned from their casual attitudes and gave their attention to the wall of leaves standing at the end of the main
wide pathway. There was a clipped narrow corridor in
front of the wall and from it emerged a happy band of naked children. They advanced slowly and disorderly, strew-
ing the path with tiny pink petals that they lifted out in
dripping handfuls from woven baskets slung over their
shoulders. They were singing in unison, but Linnaeus could
not make out the melody, their soprano voices pitched beyond his range of hearing. Following the children came another group of musicians, blowing and thumping, and then
a train of comely maidens, dressed in airy long white
dresses tied about the waists with broad ribbons, green and
yellow. The maidens, too, were singing, and the botanist
now began to hear the vocal music, a measured but joyous
choral hymn. Linnaeus was smiling to himself, buoyed up
on an ocean of happy fullness; his face and eyes were
bright.

The beautiful maidens were followed by another troop of petal-scattering children, and after them came a large orderly group of animals of all sorts, domestic animals and wild animals and fantastic animals, stalking forward with their fine innate dignities, though not, of course, in step. The animals were unattended, moving in the procession as if conscious of their places and duties. There were more of these animals, male and female of each kind, than Linnaeus had expected to live within the plant. He attempted vainly to count the number of different species, but he gave over as they kept pouring forward smoothly, like sand grains twinkling into the bottom of an hourglass.

The spectators had gathered to the sides of the pathway and stood cheering and applauding.

The animals passed by, and now a train of carriages ranked in twos took their place. These carriages each were drawn by teams of four little horses, and both the horses and carriages were loaded down with great garlands of bright flowers, hung with blooms from end to end. Powdered ladies fluttered their fans in the windows. And after the carriages, another band of musicians marched.

Slowly now, little by little, a large company of strong young men appeared, scores of them. Each wore a stout leather harness from which long reins of leather were attached behind to an enormous wheeled platform. The young men, their bodies shining, drew this platform down the pathway. The platform itself supported another formal garden, within which was an interior arrangement suggestive of a royal court. There was a throne on its dais, and numerous attendants before and behind the throne. Flaming braziers in each corner gave off thick grayish-purple clouds of smoke, and around these braziers small children exhibited various instruments and implements connected with the science of botany: shovels, thermometers, barometers, potting spades, and so forth. Below the dais on the left-hand side, a savage, a New World Indian, adorned with feathers and gold, knelt in homage, and in front of him a

beautiful woman in Turkish dress proffered to the throne a
tea shrub in a silver pot. Farther to the left, at the edge of
the tableau, a sable Ethiopian stood, he also carrying a
plant indigenous to his mysterious continent.

The throne itself was a living creature, a great tawny lion
with sherry-colored eyes. The power and wildness of the
creature were unmistakable in him, but now he lay placid
and willing, with a sleepy smile on his face. And on this
throne of the living lion, over whose back a covering of
deep-plush green satin had been thrown, sat the goddess
Flora. This was she indeed, wearing a golden crown and
holding in her left hand a gathering of peonies (*Paeonia
officinalis*) and in her right hand a heavy golden key. Flora
sat in ease, the goddess gowned in a carmine silk that
shone silver where the light fell on it in broad planes, the
gown tied over her right shoulder and arm to form a sleeve,
and gathered lower on her left side to leave the breast bare.
An expression of sublime dreaminess was on her face and
she gazed off into a far distance, thinking thoughts un-
knowable even to her most intimate initiates. She was attended on her right-hand side by Apollo, splendidly naked
except for the laurel bays round his forehead and his bow
and quiver crossed on his chest. Behind her Diana disposed
herself, half-reclining, half-supporting herself on her bow,
and wearing in her hair her crescent-moon fillet. Apollo
devoted his attention to Flora, holding aloft a blazing torch,
and looking down upon her with an expression of mingled
tenderness and admiration. He stood astride the carcass of
a loathsome slain dragon, signifying the demise of igno-
rance and superstitious unbelief.

The music rolled forth in loud hosannas, and the spectators on every side knelt in reverence to the goddess as she
passed.

Linnaeus became dizzy. He closed his eyes for a moment
and felt the floor twirling beneath his feet. He stumbled
across the room to his chair by the writing table and sat.
His chin dropped down on his chest; he fell into a deep
swoon.

When he regained consciousness, the shaft of sunlight had reached the west wall. At least an hour had passed. When he stirred himself, there was an unaccustomed stiffness in his limbs and it seemed to him that over the past twenty-four hours or so his body had aged several years.

His first clear thoughts were of the plant, and he rose and went to his worktable to find out what changes had occurred. But the plant was no more; it had disappeared. Here was the wicker container lined with oilcloth, here was the earth inside it, now returned to its dry and crumbly condition, but the wonderful plant no longer existed. All that remained was a greasy gray-green powder sifted over the soil. Linnaeus took up a pinch of it in his fingers and sniffed at it and even tasted it, but it had no sensory qualities at all except a neutral oiliness. Absentmindedly he wiped his fingers on his coat sleeve.

A deep melancholy descended upon the man and he locked his hands behind his back and began walking about the room, striding up and down beside his worktable. A harsh welter of thoughts and impulses overcame his mind. At one point he halted in mid-stride, turned and crossed to his writing table, and snatched up his journal, anxious to determine what account he had written of his strange adventure.

His journal was no help at all, for he could not read it. He looked at the unfinished last page and then thumbed backward for seven pages and turned them all over again, staring and staring. He had written in a script unintelligible to him, a writing that seemed to bear some distant resemblance to Arabic perhaps, but which bore no resemblance at all to his usual exuberant mixture of Latin and Swedish. Not a word or a syllable on any page conveyed the least meaning to him.

As he gazed at these dots and squiggles he had scratched on the page, Linnaeus began to forget. He waved his hand before his face like a man brushing away cobwebs. The more he looked at his pages, the more he forgot, until fi-

nally he had forgotten the whole episode: the letter from
the Dutch sailor, the receiving of the plant, the discovery
of the little world the plant contained—everything.

Like a man in a trance, and with entranced movements,
he returned to his worktable and swept some scattered
crumbs of soil into a broken pot and carried it away and
deposited it in the dustbin.

It has been said that some great minds have the ability *to
forget deeply*. That is what happened to Linnaeus; he forgot
the plant and the bright vision that had been vouchsafed
to him. But the profoundest levels of his life had been
stirred, and some of the details of his thinking had
changed.

His love for metaphor sharpened, for one thing. Writing
in his *Deliciae naturae*, which appeared fourteen years after
his encounter with the plant, he described a small pink-
flowered ericaceous plant of Lapland growing on a rock
by a pool, with a newt as "the blushing naked princess
Andromeda, lovable and beautiful, chained to a sea rock
and exposed to a horrible dragon." These kinds of conceits
intrigued him, and more than ever metaphor began to in-
form the way he perceived and outlined the facts of his
science.

Another happy change in his life was the cessation of his
bad nights of sleeplessness and uneasy dreams. No longer
was he troubled by memories of the attacks of Siegesbeck
or any other of his old opponents. Linnaeus had acquired
a new and resistless faith in his observations. He was finally
certain that the plants of this earth carry on their love affairs in uncaring merry freedom, making whatever sexual
arrangements best suit them, and that they go to replenish
the globe guiltlessly, in high and winsome delight.

LADIES FROM LAPLAND

 Once fired, passion for the philosophy of Isaac Newton proved unquenchable in Europe. The celebrated Émilie
Du Châtelet provides an example of enthusiasm. She was so
engrossed in writing her treatise of Newton that she would
not leave off even to bear her child, and this daughter was
born there in her study and laid in linen on a large-folio geometry text. Not many days afterward, Mme. Du Châtelet
herself was laid in the severer angles of her grave.

The famous savant had first heard of Newton from a
quick-tempered and rather acid savant named Pierre Louis
Moreau de Maupertuis. Maupertuis began as one of those
child prodigies whom we may find either charming or detestable; at the age of six he desired to know why the same
wind that extinguishes a candle flame serves to make a fire
grow roaring. It was during his leisure hours as an officer
in the Gray Musketeers that he trained himself as a scien-
tist-philosopher.

As much for his malicious wit as for intellectual achievement, he established such reputation that he was highly favored by the learned ladies of the 1720s, and Mme. Du Châtelet employed him as her geometry tutor. Immediately there was rumor they were lovers, and why should they not be? Maupertuis reserved his angry jests for his male rivals and was willing and complaisant among the females; Mme. Du Châtelet had amorous desires to match the fierceness of her intellectual desires. In fact, it was the urgency of her physical need that led her from the cooling embraces of the preoccupied Voltaire to the comely but butterfly-minded Marquis de Saint-Lambert, who gave her the child that was her death.

But this was an age when honors could not long stand without a basis of solid accomplishment, and Maupertuis, who was as hungry for fame as Émilie for love, conceived the notion of establishing the first physical proof of Newton's theory of gravitation. It was thought that if any part of Newton could be demonstrated physically, the whole of the system, constructed with such rigorous consistency, must be taken as fact.

One of the corollaries of the theory of gravitation was that the earth is not perfectly round but, rather, an oblate spheroid, larger around the tropic zones and slightly flattened at the poles. So that a Huygens clock sitting on the equator, and thus farther from the center of gravity, would have to shorten its pendulum in order to keep time with an identical clock in Paris. Maupertuis proposed to test this notion by taking measurement of the earth. He would head an expedition to the polar circle and measure a degree of the meridian, while another expedition would journey to the equator for the same purpose. Gravitational experiments could be carried out that might corroborate the earlier findings of Jean Richer at Cayenne.

This is why we see, when we look at a contemporary engraved portrait of Maupertuis, in the predella below, the figure of a man, bundled in a sleigh like a baby in a cradle, and urging on a reindeer with a menacing bullwhip. This is Maupertuis, intrepid in the icy vastness, rushing to the end of the world, anxious to triangulate and compute.

The device is merely emblematic. His colleagues in the expedition—Clairaut, Outhier, Camus, and Le Monnier—complained that they lumbered about in the snow with the bulky instruments while Maupertuis did little of the work or none.

Yet he was not idle. There were women in Lapland, as there must be in every society upon the earth, and when Maupertuis caught sight of these small round-faced ladies with their shiny black hair and their eyes dark and trusting, his thoughts ranged far from gnomons and clocks and Newton.

He looked at the Lapland women and thought that here, too, was a terra incognita from which he could learn things unknown in Europe. And it was a territory to which he could bring enlightenment, and he began to imagine himself as a missionary, cultivating the civilized arts of love in an untutored land where the nighttime went on for months. Was ever such opportunity given a man? He thought of Ovid in exile, bringing the amatory practices of Rome to the rude provincials. He thought of many things.

He was utterly charmed by these women who gathered round him, marveling at the whiteness of his complexion and his strange clothing. They reached out to touch him, tugging like curious children at his hands and waistcoat and breeches. They murmured liquidly like quail; they looked at one another and giggled.

The Lapland men stood apart, smiling in friendly fashion, shier than the women, but with a reserve of dignity.

Maupertuis wasted no time. As soon as lodgings were set up—large round reindeer-skin tents open at the top—and the other members of the expedition set off to capture angles and degrees, the famous scientist invited two of the prettiest and shiest of the women (sisters, as it turned out) to take supper with him in the main tent. He spoke to them in French and accompanied his invitation with the full

panoply of Continental gallantry, sweeping bows, bended
knees, hand kissing, and so forth. The sisters, at first
alarmed, became amused and burst into melodious laughter. Maupertuis felt confident that he had made himself understood, and he retired to prepare.

When the sisters arrived a little past the appointed time,
an astonishing spectacle met their eyes. The air inside the
geometrician's tent smelled not of burning tallow but
sweetly, as of uncountable flowers. The round shell of
cured hide was hung with gauzy drapery that stirred lan-
guorously as they opened the tent flap. Maupertuis had
spared no expense. Two bound racks of reindeer antlers
hung suspended from the tent poles and on each antler
point was flaming a precious wax candle: a crude arrangement, but still a chandelier. It was the most light these ladies had ever seen, except for the light of the summer sun.
The geometrician had undergone a transformation, dressed
now in stiff rich cloth with glittering yellow buttons and
large stiff frills at his wrists. His face had grown even paler
than before except for two large red spots on his cheeks.

The sisters were struck with wonder and gazed about as
if they could never see enough of these strange sights.
When Maupertuis motioned for them to seat themselves,
they huddled together on a bench over which woolen lap
robes had been thrown, and clutched each other's hands.
They were numb with amazement; they could not speak.

The sisters seemed to have been transfigured also, for
their names had changed. Ainu found herself being addressed as Mademoiselle Choufleur and Tsalma as Mademoiselle Doucette, these titles accompanied by Maupertuis's
exaggerated bowings and genuflections.

The ghostly-looking man drew up a bench and sat before
them, chattering away in French and gesticulating languidly. He smiled continually. He looked first deep into the
eyes of Mlle. Doucette and then into Mlle. Choufleur's
eyes; then he looked away coyly, like a child with a
naughty secret. He rose and went to the other side of the

tent and brought two sparkling crystal glasses for the sisters and one for himself, and he filled the three glasses red from a bottle.

The sisters had never taken wine and at first did not like it. But in the interest of good manners they emptied their glasses a number of times, to find that Maupertuis always replenished them. They grew warm and exhilarated and by way of experiment attempted to imitate some of the sounds their host poured out in gushing profusion. These primitive tries at the French language delighted Maupertuis and he became more voluble than ever. Tsalma fumbled with her new name, "Mzelle Dooz't," and these words so excited Maupertuis that he leapt up and kissed her on both cheeks. His eyes were brighter now and his breath quickened. She was covered with confusion and clapped her hands over her eyes.

He then produced a platter of strange foods, biscuits and jellies and sweetmeats, and prevailed upon the ladies to experiment. They were wild as children for these delicacies, and Mlle. Choufleur's mouth and chin were colorfully smeared with jam, and her fingers, too, as she ate the sweets as a bear would eat honey. This gave Maupertuis reason to kiss her on the mouth and, not content with this pleasantry, he began to lick her face. She laughed and her sister laughed and also began to lick her face.

An elaborate and exhilarating game developed, the three of them smearing and licking, smacking their lips and kissing one another repeatedly. All was proceeding more smoothly than Maupertuis had anticipated. The tent was quite warm, the sisters heated with wine, and the scientist encountered little resistance in divesting them first of their long fur waistcoats and then of their sealskin trousers. Gravely and ceremoniously, Maupertuis bared himself to the waist, retaining for the moment his linen breeches. But the sisters were naked, except for Doucette, who had found in an open trunk a wig. Maupertuis helped her to don it, and Choufleur and the Frenchman burst into hilarious laughter.

Doucette stood, this lovely woman with skin the color of

darkened bone and her round face merry and astonished and her small dark-nippled breasts bare, before them, the silver wig as incongruous on her brow as the golden helmet of Mambrino. She uttered some sounds, which she must have intended to sound like French, and attempted a low bow in the manner of her new friend. The wig fell at his feet, and then Doucette fell between the other two, who were now seated on the bench. She was laughing so heartily, she could not even breathe, and Maupertuis began to pat and caress her bare shoulder. Doucette turned her head to peer up at him, and her face was full of impudent mischief.

The sisters once more became intrigued with the strange whiteness of his skin and began to examine closely his chest and back and arms, tugging at his flesh like puppies. Their curiosity was aroused and they pulled at his breeches, anxious to determine whether his nether parts were as snowily French as the rest of him. Nothing loath, Maupertuis joined them in nudity, and seemed to show as great an interest in their bodies as they in his.

In fact, he thought that he had never seen figures so perfectly formed, such charming dusky beauty. Their faces, shoulders, breasts, and hips were of a delectable symmetrical roundness. They were not all covered with savage hair as he had imagined; even the pubic hair was contained in a small neat triangle as delicate as Alençon lace. Very striking, too, was the gleaming whiteness of their perfect teeth, set against so much loveliness tinged with shadow.

By degree and degree, Maupertuis allowed his investigations to become less anthropological and more personal. The ladies, who had at first exhibited no special interest in his penis, became delightedly intent as it began to manifest an independent spirit, and now made it the focal point of their pullings and pokings.

He rose to his feet and with due gravity flung a large fur lap robe down beside the fire in the middle space. He took Mlle. Doucette's hand solemnly and led her to couch upon it. He knelt above her and parted her legs gently, but before beginning any part of his maneuvers, he turned to smile encouragingly at Mlle. Choufleur, and beckoned her to join them. She smiled but looked aside modestly.

Maupertuis from the first had intended by way of experiment *de faire Minette* with a woman of Lapland, and when he crept between her legs and commenced those operations with mouth and tongue that were so widely appreciated in Paris, Mlle. Doucette burst into uncontrollable laughter, like a child being tickled along the ribs. This was rather disconcerting for Maupertuis, but he had expected resistance of some sort and was determined to carry out his project. He was possessed, after all, of the patience of the geometer, and, stretching his arms upward to clasp her breasts, continued in his delicate task. He was surprised to find that Doucette did not taste of rancid tallow and seal blubber but was reminiscent of cool ferns and clear springwater.

Maupertuis persisted in the familiar practice until Doucette's resistance gave way and the power of Venus held sway over her blood. She gasped openmouthed in delight and after a while found herself brought to that condition that eighteenth-century diction renders in such terms as *transports of joy, effusions of balm, heights of ecstasy,* and so forth. Afterward, when she had somewhat recollected herself, she gazed at Maupertuis with an expression of submissive adoration.

But this episode hardly had allayed Maupertuis's own fervor. Now he enticed—it took no special pleading, to be sure—Mlle. Choufleur to the selfsame trysting spot and they began to make love in more ordinary fashion, in ways recognizable even in Lapland. Highly satisfactory it was, too, to the representatives of both exotic cultures.

The ladies were astonished to learn, however, that this was not the end of their amorous merrymaking. The scientist was not content to be satisfied; he must be sated. And so the sportive pursuit began all over again, this time in a more tender and deliberate motion and at a slower tempo, and involving all three of them. A sweet languor character-

ized their movements and they dallied thoughtfully, like
figures in a reverie on a long summer afternoon.

Gradually the night's encounter came to an end. The sisters' warm dark eyes were dulled, as if they were under
the influence of narcotics. They warbled softly in Lapp and
insisted on covering Maupertuis with kisses once
more—his arms, chest, hands, even his knobbled knees.
Doucette rubbed reflectively at the patches of red on her
inner thigh where Maupertuis's face rouge had come off.
Her finger came away painted with rouge and she put it
into her mouth.

With drowsy lassitude, and regretfully, the three of them
put on their clothes. They stroked one another and murmured endearments. Finally, with slow reluctance, the sisters took their leave. They had duties to attend, though
Maupertuis did not know what these duties might be. In
truth, he did not much care. His active spirits were in abey-
ance; he did not wish to think of the morrow. He stood for
a long moment at the open tent flap as the sisters disappeared into the dimness.

When he came back to the fire, though, he began to re-
vive a bit. He had met such degree of success as he had
hardly dared to hope for, and how was there any way his
researches should not continue? Why should they meet
with any less success in the future? He sank tiredly onto a
bench and looked into the orange heart of the sinking fire
and smiled the smile of reason.

The fame of Maupertuis's pleasure tent spread rapidly. The
number of his female visitants must have been prodigious;
rumor imputes upward of a dozen at a time, but surely this
number is unlikely. The numbers were undeterminable.
Who can, or would, be accurate in these circumstances?
But there must have been crowds of yielding ladies, for
after some weeks even the most obliging of the Lapland
men began to show signs of restiveness.

Maupertuis's colleagues were thoroughly displeased.

Their leader had aided hardly at all in taking measurements, and contented himself with totting up columns of figures and with commenting, often sardonically, upon the quality of their labors. Clairaut especially, among the other scientists, was bent on painting Maupertuis in his true colors when once they returned to civilization.

Perhaps it was Clairaut's determination to expose Maupertuis that was as responsible as any other factor for the swift and triumphant completion of the project. All was finished on schedule, and the scientists were ready to return to Paris, there to await the arrival of La Condamine from Peru, where he had gone to measure the equator. Word had reached them that the Peruvian expedition had been plagued with harsh and even tragic difficulty, but that La Condamine would persist and overcome.

Here in Lapland there was a different sort of difficulty regarding departure. The ladies of Lapland were heartbroken to hear that Maupertuis was on point of leaving. Individually and in hastily assembled groups, they invented every possible allurement to keep him here at the top of the world. The philosopher explained over and over again that his work here was ended, that he had a duty to science, that generations unborn would share his gratitude toward the Laplanders for their gracious hospitality.

It occurred to the ladies that if he would not stay, they would go with him, all the way to the wilderness of Paris; they could not bear to be without him. Even as Maupertuis was demonstrating to them that this fantasy was impossible of fulfillment, the memory of desire came over him and he relented so far as to agree to take four—only four—of the women to France. He would choose. There was to be no violence, no lamenting, no unseemly display; they were to abide compliantly by his decision. He went among them like a housewife selecting vegetables from the market and chose four comely companions to journey with him and taste the gratifications of silken hose and chocolate gâteaux. Incurably sentimental, he included among these four

his old friends Mlle. Choufleur and Mlle. Doucette. He
then, with awkward speed, made ready to embark.

Clairaut and the others at first were furiously angered by
Maupertuis's decision to carry back these living specimens
of polar fauna, but then they realized that their wayward
leader was taking to Paris the very evidence that would
damn him and justify their accusations of negligence and
knavery. At the hour of departure they were so thoroughly
reconciled to the venture that they applied themselves to
assist the ladies in all possible ways.

As the ship pulled away from the icy shores, Maupertuis
thought that he heard in the wind a wailing as of tribes
of bereaved women. He shook his head to clear away this
delusion.

The homeward journey was terrifying, bad diet and foul
weather. They endured shipwreck off the coast of Norway,
an incident that Maupertuis, in ensuing years, wrought out
in such heroic terms that Voltaire felt constrained to make
angry mock of it in his *Micromégas*. The four Lapland ladies
were continually frightened and bewildered and clung to
Maupertuis as threatened children to their mother.

But the philosopher was in process of making a surprising and disappointing discovery. The farther the four
women traveled from their snowy homeland, the more
their beauties suffered diminishment. Their complexions,
which by firelight and lamplight in the tent had appeared
as the quality of old ivory, now seemed dun and dingy.
The delicious small roundness that had made their figures
so attractive had become a squat dumpiness. Their formerly
amusing attempts at French sounded like the irritable chat-
ter of apes. And even their teeth seemed to have lost
dazzle.

By the time the ship made port at Le Havre, Maupertuis
was thoroughly disillusioned. He began to conceive that he
would be seen a laughingstock, and this above all other
things he could not bear. There was danger, too, that the

exotic presence of these females would draw attention away from the scientific value of the expedition, and that his merited reputation would be occluded by the atmosphere of the raree-show.

After half an hour of restless and regretful cogitation, Maupertuis decided to abandon these ladies as soon as the company arrived in Paris. Or if he did not abandon them, he would find ways to keep them hidden away, at least until the time that his scientific endeavors had garnered due recognition.

He ended, of course, by abandoning them. It was left to Clairaut to minister after this further piece of reckless impertinence. He arranged a house for the four of them in one of the less frequented quarters of the city and gave them what assistance he could in adjusting to the rigors of civilization. At a later date he was able to obtain for them a small but sufficient royal pension.

Maupertuis had accomplished his grand scheme and had experienced no tarnishing. He went from glory to glory, recounting his adventures, explaining the importance of his newly proven theories, strutting about like a young bravo with his first challenge to duel. He turned up at the Café Gradot, that favorite haunt of astronomers and mathematicians, sweating under the full bulk of his Lapland costume. His accomplishment was universally bruited, and his face was known everywhere, especially after the broad dissemination of the famous engraving taken after the painting by Tournières.

Mme. Graffigny, another celebrated savant, was excited to have come upon this engraving. She was slightly acquainted with Clairaut and wrote to congratulate him upon his close association with the great man. She described the engraving closely, the reindeer and sleigh in the predella, and the figure of Maupertuis above, pointing with his left hand toward the marvelous unknown future, while his right hand pressed down on a figure of the globe of the world, flattening it slightly at the poles. *Globe-flattener* had, in fact, become Maupertuis's fond public sobriquet.

In answering the letter, Clairaut, after tendering his affectionate respect, desired her to look more carefully at the representation of that globe, to make certain it was not a woman's breast beneath the hand of Maupertuis. He then went on to tell the whole story, assuring her that it could be verified by a visit to number 44, rue de l'Eplatisseur.

Mme. Graffigny wasted no time in making her visit, accompanied by an intellectual friend. She found the situation to be more or less as Clairaut had reported, though he had not indicated the full range of strangeness and contradiction. Here were the four Lapland ladies, lonely and dispirited, quarreling spitefully in a debased and raucous tongue. They were dressed in fashionable gowns that in no way could contain their capacious hips and upper arms. No shoemaker stocked a last to fit them, and they flopped about in soiled carpet slippers. Wigs they wore, too, monstrous high-piled wigs they were immoderately proud of; but these would not sit straight and kept sliding down over their eyes. By this time the splendid Lapland teeth were ruinous, as the ladies partook incessantly of cakes, confits, sweetmeats, and syrups. Mme. Graffigny visited with them for two hours, learning what she could, but left the house with such feeling of relief that she was never to return.

She described in one of her many voluminous letters to M. "Panpan" Devaux some of the details of her visit. "You will not be sorry to hear, my dear friend," she began, "that our love-attracting Frenchmen please even in frozen climates, and that love is of every country." She went on in her usual way to make an entrancing narrative of the episode, telling of the many oddities and vanities, and of the general ridiculousness, of these strange women. Maupertuis's secret was abroad now, and Mme. Graffigny concluded her account by saying, "All Paris goes to that house to see the Lapp ladies. Ah, mon Dieu, how can one be a Laplander?"

THE SNOW THAT IS

NOTHING IN THE

TRIANGLE

 "If we construct, gentlemen, an equilateral triangle
on a sheet of paper, an ordinary sheet of paper such as we
customarily use, what is in the triangle?"

They replied with silence, their faces troubled. Nothing
is in the triangle. What did Herr Professor Feuerbach want
his students to answer? In the minds of these clever young
men was the vivid memory of the time their professor
marched into the classroom with a sword unsheathed,
threatening in all seriousness to behead those who could
not solve the problem he would propose. Things were not
well with Feuerbach, but his students did not know why.

"You will say: Nothing," he continued. "You will say that nothing is in the triangle, but that is wrong. The correct answer is: Snow. It is snow inside the triangle."

Snow. They looked at one another in distress, but when he asked them to repeat the word, they obeyed compliantly.

Snow.

They looked at his dirty white hair, dressed loosely in the old long fashion, falling in raddled strings on his shoulders. If it was ever washed, his thin greasy hair would be as white as the moon, and his fingernails were long and horny like those of a man of ninety years, when the hand begins to look like an object no longer entirely human. Yet he was young, not so much older than his students, the youngest man ever appointed to such a position here at the Gymnasium in Erlangen.

"Ah, but wait. You will not be completely mistaken, either. For if snow is nothing, it is yet a Substantive Nothing. Suppose a man were to plunge into a snowbank up to his neck, or even over his head. Will we then say that he has fallen into Nothing?" He nodded heavily, in sage agreement with himself. "Yes. He has fallen into Nothing, and who can tell what consequences will ensue?" He looked about, pleading. "Who can tell us that?"

They no longer called him the Pope of the Theorems, as they used to do, referring to his pontifical brilliance as a teacher of geometry and to his physique. His body, like that of the famous English poet of seventy years past, was crushed into the shape of a question mark and he hobbled about in obvious pain, scurrying and halting like a crab. But his manner had become so odd that students now called him only Feuerbach, his name descriptive beyond the power of adjectives. For a brief period they called him old Feuerbach, only to discover that his age was but thirty-two. But finally he was no age at all; he existed outside time, like a topological proposition that has never been proven.

"Yes, it is true that it is snow in our constructed triangle, but, gentlemen, please do me the service of keeping quiet upon this matter. It is to be our secret." As soon as he uttered the word *secret*, with a queer hushed emphasis, he began to look about the classroom apprehensively. Then, with a sudden expression of alarm, he crossed to the door and flung it open. The hallway was empty, but he looked up and down with the closest scrutiny, as if suspecting that something escaped his survey.

The students shifted in their seats. Every day it became harder to remember that their own Herr Professor was the same man who had produced the most beautiful theorem in plane geometry since the time of Euclid. It bore his name, the Feuerbach Theorem. "For any triangle, the nine-point circle is tangent to the in-circle and to each of the three ex-circles of the triangle." There was a lovely corollary also, because the nine-point circle passes through the three feet of the altitudes of the triangle and the three points bisecting the joins of the orthocenter to the three vertices. This was a theorem so elegant that some wonder-struck students had decorated the flyleaves of their textbooks with drawings of it.

Now Feuerbach trotted back and perched his R-shaped body on the edge of the desk. "Secret secret secret," he cooed. He leaned forward in order to engage them in earnest confidentiality. "This is another word that, gentlemen, you must never utter. Do you know why?"

He waited for their answer; they waited for his.

"Because it is destructive to your health. Observe, please, my body, gentlemen. You will see that I am not blessed with the form of an Apollo, but twisted like a curve in space. That is because of the word *secret*. It is easy to demonstrate step by step the linkage between the word *secret* and the prison cell and the triangle full of snow which is Nothing." His voice had subsided to a raspy whisper like the sound of a distant cicada and he leaned so far forward that they feared he might tumble from the desk. "Gentle-

men, gentlemen. You may try to cut the veins in your feet,
but they will not allow you to die. No, you cannot bleed
to death in that manner, for there is a guard who coughs
and shuffles in the corridor coming to your door and then
they take you to the infirmary and bind up the veins again
and then you are alive after all. There are twenty of you,
they say. There are twenty of you, but only one may die,
that much is clear. Observe, please. I will demonstrate."
    He hopped to the floor and limped to the blackboard. He
seized a piece of chalk, but there was no space in which to
write. He had already covered the board with partial constructions, numbers, mottoes, Greek and Latin abbrevia-
tions, scraps of poetry, and curious squiggles. He stood
looking at this wilderness of scrawl in bafflement.
    He turned on his heel back toward the class and indi-
cated the whole of the board with a languid sweep of his
hand. "Klaus Hörnli will now solve this problem," he said.
    The eleven students looked at one another. Finally one
of them dared to say, "There is no Klaus Hörnli among us,
Herr Professor."
    He laid down the chalk and rubbed his hands together.
"So then. You see. By now it is evident; it is as evident as
sunlight, is it not? There is no Klaus Hörnli among us." His
voice quavered and his cheek trembled with irrepressible
sorrow. "And he was the best of us, gentlemen, markedly
the best." He wiped a tear, then brightened. "But this con-
stitutes our proof, does it not? Klaus is absent while I am
here. The snow that is Nothing in the triangle has rejected
me, but has accepted Klaus. Q. E. D., gentlemen. This is
clear, as clear as sunlight."
    Again the student ventured to demur. "Herr Professor, I
am afraid that we do not completely understand."
    "How can you not understand? It is evident as sunlight.
Any fool can understand. Even an idiot, a madman."
Anger stopped his voice in his throat and his face burned
red. He coughed repeatedly. His whole body shuddered
convulsively, as if it might tear apart, then settled. A peace-

ful gravity took possession; his expression softened and his
eyes were wise and wet.

"We will begin again from the beginning." His tone was
mild, reasonable, wondering. "Two young men are walking along the street. An ordinary day with clouds in the
sky, and two young men walking along, chatting as perhaps any of you gentlemen might be chatting with one of
your friends."

He paused and peered anxiously into their faces. "Do
you comprehend our axiom? Do you understand how we
must begin?" Klaus Hörnli was the young man in Feuerbach's company. Blond Klaus, high-spirited, witty, and sar-
donic as it is in the character of brilliant young students to
be, when suddenly two officers of the court, two agents,
rather, in dark unseasonable overcoats, you could not have
known them for police agents, you could not decipher, decipher. "Gentlemen, how could a geometrician be an anarchist? Is not anarchy disorder? But do not the propositions
of Euclid follow as inevitably from one another as the roses
spring from the vine? I include even the famous troublesome fifth proposition, gentlemen. Let us begin once more
with our axiom. Two young men walking, and let us propose that the town is Hof, wealthy and respected and with
a reputable Gymnasium." Anarchos, meaning without a
ruler, there can be no construction without a ruler, he
Klaus Hörnli was no anarchist, he Karl Feuerbach was no
anarchist. "Gentlemen, you must not take the loose and
spirited talk of students in the beer gardens for plots and
conspiracies, that is a false conclusion, as I will now demonstrate."

He went back to the blackboard and searched diligently
for the chalk without finding it, meanwhile they were
questioned endlessly, taken from their cells and asked to
elucidate faulty propositions without being given the necessary axioms. There was a guard or there were many guards
who paced the corridor outside the battered doors of the
cells, all these turnkeys in poor health, coughing snuffling

sputtering, racking their weakened lungs for blobs of
phlegm to swallow down again, shuffling their feet along
with the slithery sound of worn-away leather, a sound that
kept erasing the thoughts of him Hörnli Feuerbach inside
the cell, the shuffled feet wiping out the clear mathematical
propositions. A hexagon would appear to him, shining
white on a black background, on black paper, and then the
feet would come shuffling and the hexagon would disappear. That was in early autumn, the first autumn in the
prison cell, and when the snows began, the sound, the
sound of the snow falling, was quite loud, louder than you
would ever expect, a sound like the shuffling of the feet of
the many turnkeys there in the corridor, the snow that fell
into the interiors of any closed construction, square rectangle circle triangle, and filled it up with the sound of shuffling, the lines no longer discernible on the black paper
covered with snow.

Feuerbach flapped his arms helplessly at the blackboard
and all its notation, then turned around and came back
into his cell, dark there in the cells and the bitter cold, and
many of us fell ill, there were twenty of us all told. "Do
you understand, gentlemen, that there would be from a
group of twenty one by one, or as it may be in some cases,
by twos and threes, distracted or abstracted or subtracted
from the cardinal order of their lives?" And clapped into
cells by slow heavy featureless men in the dark coats and
overlooked by foul tubercular guards and ordered to fabri-
cate in a pitiless given period of time and without any materials a geometry of anarchy. "The mind is not anarchical.
Gentlemen, it is not. For instance, geometry as it occurs in
nature, the snowflake, let us say, with its infinitely varying
but unvarying hexagon, is clear proof that the mind is not
anarchical and contains within itself all the shapes of geometry which it does not require that nature supply, yet
here in the snowflake nature reaches out to us as if it were
reassuringly, gentlemen, suggesting that the mind makes
no mistake in intuiting intimations of a high and eternal

order, an order that, though we can but guess at it, is as certain and apprehensible as the Pythagorean theorem."

But then all the little hexagons of the snow filled up the larger construction in the mind with the sounds of coughing and shuffling until by minute gradations, gradually gradually, you understand, the Concluding Proposition began to show clear, to appear in burning letters in his mind on the black paper, melting away the accumulation of snow with letters of yellow fire: IF ONE MAN DIE, THE OTHERS SHALL BE FREED.

There was no doubting this intuition written in the pure element of fire, appearing in the way that such intuitions must have come in antique time to Plato, to Euclid, to Aristotle, and no doubt either of the further corollary, that he Karl Wilhelm Feuerbach must be the man to die, as the cough and shuffle of the snow hexagons fell upon the burning letters but could not quench them, melting away in space above the black page in his mind with its letters of yellow flame, and so . . .

Feuerbach began to weep and turned away suddenly from the students to wipe his eyes on his sleeve, not being able to locate his handkerchief, it being taken away from him by the turnkey along with his chalk, and he was making a spectacle of himself and giving the students to conjecture that geometry is a cause for weeping. "You must understand, gentlemen, you must forgive, we must all learn to understand and to forgive." And so

he cut the veins in his feet, or sawed them, as it is more accurate to say, slowly and painfully with a bit of ragged dull metal he had gotten, and it disturbed him now that he could not remember where he had gotten that little bit of metal and so began to weep afresh and turned away again, for he could not bear that high-spirited Klaus Hörnli smiling as he always smiled cheerfully in the last row of the classroom would see him weeping when he Feuerbach had so much less reason for tears than Klaus who was after all dead, Feuerbach must keep it in mind that Klaus had died,

accepted into the Triangle Nothingness, while he Feuerbach
had been rejected.

It was the medal with the portrait of Euclid he had won
as a school prize and kept on a little silver chain around
his neck, the mathematics prize he had won in fifth form,
the medal he had kept on scraping against the stone wall
of his cell, honing honing until he had achieved an edge
not very satisfactory, no keenness. "No, gentlemen, you
could not say of it that it possessed any degree of keenness,
you would not call it sharp," and so

had managed at last to saw through the veins in his feet
and lay back to die, and so

now they would free the others, Feuerbach's death a
surety for their innocence of all political charges, and now
he remembered and his feet began to hurt and he hopped
up backward to sit on the desk and hold his left foot in
both hands, cooing to it as a mother to her child, "gentlemen gentlemen gentlemen," but as the snow of sleep
drifted down to settle on the letters in his mind and now
finally not melting away but covering over the letters he
closed his eyes and tried not to sleep but the snow kept
coming down, heavy, gray snow like greasy ash, snow as
sleepy as it was heavy, as warm as it was cold, and then the
burning letters he could no longer see though they must be
burning still somewhere in space, and then

he awoke. Oh God. In the infirmary he awoke and it
was now a white and pure snow that was falling outside
the window across from his bed, on the sharp angles of the
roofs, on the triangles of the gables, on the curves in space
of the bare chestnut limbs, a pure white cold snow and
when he saw it he knew that

he was alive, he had not died, and when he knew that
fact

the dull sick sound of shuffling feet returned into the falling snow and in his mind on the black paper would come
no more the clean geometric constructions, and his friends
and colleagues were still in their miserable cells, and now

the greasy ash of snow melted and ran down in streams off the black paper and the letters appeared burning once more IF ONE MAN DIE, THE OTHERS SHALL BE FREED, the yellow letters hotter and brighter than before, and he turned in the narrow bed to face the infirmary wall though the movement made his feet burn as if scalded and to soak the bandages with blood, and he wept copiously and bitterly because he had not managed to die. He had failed.

"I ask you, gentlemen, did Plato and Aristotle and Euclid fail the visions that were so clearly delivered to them, appearing in their minds as sharp as letters of flame? Gentlemen, they did not. But ours is an age of pygmy cowards and grim little secrets and we are called upon to solve problems that are not rational problems. Anarchical geometry, that is no problem, gentlemen, it is but a whim of unlettered tyrants who cannot understand the proper meaning of terms. Let us not be taken in, gentlemen, by the spurious fancies of an illiberal century."

And he let go his foot as quickly as if it were a smoking coal and let it swing like a pendulum back and forth under the desk, the imperative in his mind still fresh and burning, *if one man die,* and he Feuerbach still determined to carry it out but stricken breathless by the paradox that in order to die he must first regain his health a little, and turned in his bed to stare out the infirmary window at the shuffling snow that was coughing quietly though steadily, falling on roof ridge and gable angle. If he could no longer produce clear geometric constructions in his mind, there were yet these angles in nature to be observed, the shuffling snow could soften but not obliterate them, and so he began to grow cunning, and so

very crafty he was, not speaking unless spoken to, and obeying every instruction of the doctor and of the guards, though they persisted in asking those moronic questions that were not questions. He smiled at them, gently wisely forgivingly, and little by little the season turned into deep winter, and the snow kept falling and its shuffling sound

grew always louder. "Gentlemen, it is hard to think with
so much noise in our classroom. Can you not keep quiet?
Must you always be shuffling your feet and coughing?"
and so
  he had formed a plan while winning their confidence
with his warm genial smile: One day he would stroll casually to the window there by his infirmary bed and open it
casually as if he was not thinking about what he was doing, and leap out and be killed, IF ONE MAN, and kept smil-
ingly to his plan, opened the window easily and gracefully,
and hopped up backward on the ledge in just the way he
hopped up backward to sit on his desk in the classroom,
and plunged to his death three stories below

                                    no

for as it happened in his descent through the air, with his
bed robe flapping around him like broken wings, he saw
below a triangle because he had tumbled over in space and
was falling head down, a triangle with the infirmary wall
as base and the two courtyard walls as sides, rising to meet
him with the suddenness of a geometrical intuition, a triangle without reason to exist, cramped out of the way here
behind the infirmary

"Gentlemen, it is important, nay, it is imperative, gentlemen, that we teach the designers of our buildings a proper
appreciation and knowledge of geometry so that we may
prevent such pervasively ugly and expensive public construction."

and the cruel useless triangle that rose to engulf Feuerbach
had filled up with snow during this strange long winter and
he plummeted into it, dropped into a burning pain that was
not death and which collapsed his youthful scholar's body

like a seaman's telescope

now finally the letters of yellow fire that flamed on the black page that was his mind were obliterated forever not by the snow which was Nothing but by the towering white fire that was Pain

he died but did not die in that triangle

the snow that was the Substantive Nothing had held him back from death, held him back from bringing freedom to his comrades, for when he came to himself again, when once more he was Feuerbach, they told him it was many weeks later, yet he could not think that this could be true as he lay there in the same infirmary in the same bed because

outside the window the same snow was still falling, yet he did believe, he had to believe them when they told him that Klaus Hörnli had died while he Feuerbach was dropping upward swiftly, plummeting upward out of the triangle of Substantive Nothing back to the world again, the world of dark-coated agents and coughing turnkeys from which

he Klaus Hörnli had been freed by death, his health broken in the cold slime of the cell, and of course now

now they were to be freed, Klaus's death bringing some ray of rationality to King Maximilian Joseph and even to his anarchical geometers

IF ONE MAN DIE, Feuerbach thought, but could not remember the rest of the proposition because the fire of Pain had burned away the letters of the lesser fire, but he needed to remember, it was imperative to remember, what?

He clapped his hands together repeatedly and with surprising force, the sound like a cracking of whips. "You must forgive me, gentlemen, I beg you. I feel that I may have been digressing. You must help me to recall the topic under discussion. I must rely upon your aid."

He looked at them imploringly, but how could they help him? They were strangers, and senile, these eleven old men he had never seen before. They had seated themselves in the students' chairs, and their stringy white hair was unclean and their fingernails long and horny.

"Gentlemen, I beg of you," Feuerbach said, but they would not speak and then began to shuffle their feet, a whispery sound at first that then enlarged and this sound caused an ashy gray snow to fall in the room. It fell thickly and blindly and covered the floor and the desk and the chairs and Feuerbach's hands, those hands so aged, they no longer looked entirely human.

BARCAROLE

It was in Vienna in 1871 that Jacques Offenbach made the acquaintance of Rudolf Zimmer. He was returning to his hotel from rehearsing a revival of his operetta *The Brigands*. A voluble press of citizens had spilled off the sidewalk, blocking his carriage.

The composer's curiosity was so aroused that he got down and made his way through the crowd, to find a man lying faceup on the sidewalk, icy pale and sweating and breathing harshly. When Offenbach first glimpsed the man's face, he gave a cry of dismay. It was his brother Julius, lying here sick and broken. But then he knew it was not. The man's face strongly resembled his brother's, but Julius was in Paris, enjoying good health and copying parts of a new score. Yet the likeness struck Offenbach to the heart. He knelt and put his face closely to the face of the fallen man, this stranger sick and so obviously penurious.

But if this man resembled Julius, so did Jacques, and to such degree that it might have been himself he was trying to minister to here in the open street. Except for their clothing and the signs of suffering in the stranger, it might be not two men but one man reflected as in a mirror. Either of them would present something of a spectacle, for Offenbach was extremely tall and thin and possessed a face so ugly that it never failed to charm, with an enormous lumpy nose and weak eyes behind tiny pince-nez.

Their clothing, however, offered a strong contrast. The fallen man raised his thin hand in a shabby wool coat all frayed at the cuff; his soiled linen collar, too, was frayed and his black slippers down at heel. Offenbach was dressed in the sumptuous manner in which he always strolled the boulevards. His red damask vest was enriched with gold thread, the collar of his black lamb's-wool overcoat brushed the lobes of his ears, which were almost as large as saucers. He had laid negligently on the sidewalk his top hat of rough ebony silk and his mahogany cane with its silver lion's head.

Ordinarily Offenbach would not be so careless of his clothing, for he held it an article of faith that his dress was almost as important to his career as his music. It was necessary to present himself as the most fashionable figure of café society, to be swarmed over by the butterflies and gnats of the salons, to be presented with feuilletons, album pages, score sheets, gold coins, billets-doux, and even menus, for his presence twice in one month in a café served to make it notorious in the journals for an entire season.

Someone brought a dram of brandy from a nearby brasserie and the man's head was raised and the liquor forced into his mouth. He coughed and a thread of saliva dripped from his chin. His breath rattled thinly and then he opened his eyes. The spectators exclaimed in relief and then most of them—as true Viennese—already began to turn away in pursuit of pleasure. An officious cashier from the brasserie questioned the man closely.

His name, he said, was Rudolf Zimmer. He was a musi-

cian, a violinist, and he inhabited a small apartment a few
streets away. He was not seriously ill; this was only a brief
fainting spell of the kind he had experienced before; it was
a family malady. He was embarrassed to have caused the
gentlemen alarm; he had no wish to create a scene. No,
please, no. He had no need of medical care. In his rooms
there was a medicine that had been prescribed, if they
would but help him to his feet. No, please, no. His most
earnest wish was to trouble them no longer; he was heartily ashamed. *No please no.*

But when he got to his feet, tottering, he seemed to Offenbach an entirely touching sight. He was a short man and
his thin black overcoat hung on his light frame as on a
wicker coat tree. His face was as pale as a lily and beaded
with sweat. All this, with his resemblance to brother Julius,
confused Offenbach's sympathies.

He offered to take Zimmer to his rooms at the hotel. He
was dining late alone and would be glad of the company
of a fellow musician. *Fellow musician,* he repeated, but Zimmer did not take the bait. No, please, no.

Offenbach persisted and at last Zimmer did acquiesce to
the offer of the carriage. His quarters, he said, were near
enough that he would not be taking the kind gentleman
far out of his way.

They got him in and Offenbach got in beside him and
pulled a fur robe over him up to his chin, so that in the
dim light he seemed a disembodied head, the transfigured
head of Julius—or of Jacques himself, as the thought now
struck him—murmuring avowals of gratitude. When Offenbach ascertained the directions and relayed them to the
driver, the carriage started with a lurch that rocked Zimmer's head alarmingly, like a carnival mask bobbled at the
end of a pole.

Offenbach turned to the stranger. "I will introduce myself," he said. "I am Jacques Offenbach. Of Paris."

He thought at first that his name meant nothing to the
man, for he did not reply. But then his thin lips trembled

and he turned upon his benefactor a gaze so tender, so full
of admiration, that Offenbach irresistibly thought of the
way his five sisters used to look at him as a child. There in
the tiny room in the smelly ghetto of Cologne, his sisters
would sit around him in a worshipful circle as he practiced
on his cello, that instrument he soon had mastered as thoroughly as Paganini his violin. And when he was exhausted
with exercises, scales, and arpeggios, one or the other of
his beautiful sisters would come to stand by his bed and
soothe him to sleep by humming a waltz tune, a soulful
melody that had haunted the composer all his life. He had
tried in vain for decades to track down this song, and now
the eyes of Zimmer brought these elusive strains to mind
once more.

Zimmer spoke at last. "*Il gran maestro Offenbach?* The
composer of *Orphée aux enfers*? The originator of the
cancan?"

"Yes," he replied, "though I most certainly did not in-
vent the cancan, I wrote the operetta." And he added, but
with a self-deprecating smile, "And others."

"*La Belle Hélène*," Zimmer said. "*La Vie parisienne.*"

"Yes."

Zimmer nodded. "Yes, it is you. I recognize your face
from the prints. This is a great honor for me, for poor Rudolf Zimmer."

"If you count it an honor, please let me presume upon
it to renew my offer of a supper."

"No, thank you."

"I don't mean to importune," Offenbach said, "nor to be
forward. Yet it seems to me that you are in need, perhaps
in some distress. I would be happy to aid you in any way
I can. I believe that musicians must stand together to support one another because we belong to a barely acknowl-
edged spiritual guild, one which those who are not musical
could never comprehend."

"A noble conceit, and quite worthy of you," Zimmer
said. "But I no longer think of myself as a musician, nor

even as a man. I am only the shade of a man, and so I
have been for many years."

The carriage turned off the broad Praterstrasse into a
maze of narrow streets. It was darker here and the horse's
hooves rang lonely on the cobbles. The looming houses
blocked out all but a crevice of starry sky.

"I do not understand you, Herr Zimmer."

"I know," said the shadowed man in his hoarse murmur, "that I am near the end of my life. I see all my past
and all my future laid before me as clearly as a musical
score. Everything. My destiny is so clearly written out that
I must recognize it is complete. The sonatina is finished;
the concluding fermata has been inked in."

"This is a foolish fancy caused by your illness. If only
you would come to share a bit of food with me, your view
would change and you would take heart."

"We must speak frankly," Zimmer said, "for the hour is
late. Would you like to hear the story of my life?"

"I would."

"Then I will come to you tomorrow at your hotel and
recount it. Please let me assure you, though, that it pos-
sesses not the least novelty. It is sad and sentimental and
all too predictable. Banal, perhaps. I think that a romancer
like our Herr Hoffman would cancel it from his pages,
should he ever discover that he had written a similar story.
And yet—it is true. It has that much, at least, in its favor."

"I am anxious to hear it."

"And at this street here I must take my leave," Zimmer
said. He reached out the window and rapped briskly on the
door of the carriage. When the driver halted, he opened
the door and got down with a surprising nimbleness.

"Wait," Offenbach said. "Only a moment. Please."

Zimmer bowed to the carriage. *"À demain,"* he said, and
stepped back and was lost in the darkness. It was a deeper
darkness here than Offenbach could have imagined in Vienna; there seemed about the carriage a wall of black silence. Then, after he spoke to the driver and the carriage

rattled away over the stones, the clatter of the wheels was even lonelier than before.

Offenbach entered his rooms in a state of bright confusion. A great many things were jumbled in his head, past, present, and future. The feeling that Rudolf Zimmer was strongly connected to his own past life colored his thoughts. It was more than the resemblance to Julius, more than the warmth of gaze reminiscent of his sisters; it was the powerful impression that Zimmer knew much about his personal life, even things that Offenbach himself had never known or had forgotten. Zimmer, too, was a Jew, of course, but it was unlikely that he had converted to Catholicism, as Offenbach had done.

He sighed as he stood at the sideboard to pour a glass of champagne. He glanced at the food set out there, cold fowl and veal and pâté and bread and cheese and fruit, and found he had no appetite. He could not help trying to imagine how Zimmer had made his supper: greasy cabbage soup, perhaps, with broken crusts and a thin, sour glass of claret. On his stained and peeling wall there would be a framed print of Mozart or of Beethoven or of Schubert. Maybe a print of Jacques Offenbach. Had not Zimmer mentioned that he recognized *il gran maestro* from the prints?

He thought of Zimmer's face as he had seen it in the carriage, nodding as if disembodied, and the lullaby waltz his sisters sang to him so long ago came back to haunt him now. He remembered only the first eight bars of the song, but they formed a whole world in themselves. "When they came into my mind," he would write in 1872, "I saw my father's house and heard the voices of my dear ones at home, for whom I longed." He was but twelve years old when he was exiled to Paris to earn his living as a cellist with the Opéra-Comique. "Often I found the loneliness very bitter and the waltz ended by taking enormous dimensions. It ceased to be an ordinary waltz, and became almost a prayer. When I played it, it seemed to me my dear ones heard me, and then, when it returned to my mind later, I could have sworn they were answering me."

This then was the obscure melody that had helped to create the personality that was Offenbach, the talent that gave such piquant voice to the irony and impudence of post-Napoleonic Europe. His songs celebrated the cynicism of the poor man in the street and the curdled contempt of the wealthy man in the brocade waistcoat. Policies, constitutions, and governments appeared and departed like river mists, but the music continued unhalting. Perhaps it was true, as the journals boasted, that Paris sheltered the best heads in Europe, but Offenbach wrote the cancan to exhibit the legs.

He was determined to pursue the case of Rudolf Zimmer; the inexplicable feeling that their lives were closely connected persisted to unsettling degree. He wanted to hear Zimmer's account of himself. Had not the man likened his story to a tale by E. T. A. Hoffmann? In his younger days Offenbach's physical similarity to that unhappy genius often had been remarked. In fact, it had been this resemblance that had attracted the eye of the rich and beautiful Herminie d'Alcain, the woman who was now his wife and mother of his children. He had wooed her with the composition of a lissome, plaintive waltz; "À toi," it was called, and he had dared to decorate the title page with Herminie's portrait. It was Offenbach's fortune to have even his most egregious effronteries rewarded.

But then, he reflected, one's fortune depended, too, upon the character of the time. In other decades his daring might have been considered at least bumptious and possibly dishonorable. He might have been cast out of society and a gentler, more deferential spirit ushered in to enjoy the privileges that Offenbach now enjoyed. If circumstances had been a little different in one place and opportunities had come a bit later in another, Rudolf now might be enjoying Jacques's place and Jacques Rudolf's.

This idea struck Offenbach with such dark force that he

frowned and began to disrobe in a gloomy state of mind
and afterward achieved only a restless and intermittent
night of sleep.

Zimmer did not appear at the hotel next morning as he had
promised to do. Offenbach had not expected that he would.
The composer waited, though, as long as he could and then
went off to the theater. There, as usual, he became em-
broiled in the thousand confusions of production. The set
designer and the costume designer had found themselves
at odds about the second act, and there was trouble with
the lead tenor, as there always is.

Even so, Offenbach took pains to inquire after Zimmer
and was surprised to learn that no one knew him or had
heard of him. Professional musicians generally are acquainted with one another. The poor man must have sunk
very low in life to be so thoroughly lost to sight. And Offenbach could not remember the place where Zimmer had
disembarked in the dark, silent night.

There was but one solution to this problem. A young fellow named Heinrich had attached himself to the opera
troupe, one of those carefree young people who desire no
more of the world than to be in the company of actresses
and baritones and to make themselves useful as factotums.
Because of his talent in this regard and because of his
cheerfully ambiguous sexual nature, the company had re-
named him Cherubino and looked upon him as a pet. The
management paid him a trifling sum for his services, so he
must have had another source of revenue to keep himself
so fashionably decked out. He was a willowy, water-eyed
youth with a smile for all and a remark for every occasion,
though these were often more quizzical than witty. The
chorus girls were particularly fond of Cherubino.

Offenbach called this young man into conference in his
dressing room and described the episode with Zimmer. "I
must admit," the composer said, "that he has become
something of an obsession. I am most anxious to talk with

him. Do you think you could trace him down?"

Cherubino, ever restless, spread his hands in the air and examined his fingernails. Then he put his hands into his coat pockets and took them out again. "Rudolf Zimmer," he repeated. "A fiddler. Strange old bird. In need of money. . . . When Maestro Offenbach but hints a desire, Cherubino flies to obey."

"You think that you can locate him then?"

"Within the hour."

"I should be very grateful."

"For you a small detail of a glorious life; for me a moment of signal honor." Then, looking into a space just above Offenbach's head, Cherubino began to whistle. He whistled in thin but accurate tones twelve bars of the grand waltz that Offenbach had composed in honor of the actress Rachel. He stopped abruptly, grinned nervously, bowed jerkily, and scurried away, leaving the dressing room door open behind him.

Offenbach shook his head and blinked his eyes. Here was an odd one. The world of operetta was inhabited by many extraordinary types, and it had begun to appear to the maestro that all Europe was striving to take on the character of operetta, to appropriate that milieu of fantasy and silliness as a normal mode of existence. Well, pray God that the madness of the world resulted in no more harm than a stage revue.

It seemed to him that he hardly had taken up his labors again when he was alerted that Cherubino had returned. He scribbled quickly on the French horn part he was correcting and hurried to his dressing room. There he found that Cherubino awaited him with an air of calculated insouciance, examining again his immaculate fingernails.

"Were you able to search out Herr Zimmer?" Offenbach asked.

"I have found where he lives," Cherubino replied. "I have spoken to the man in his own rooms, in his own flesh."

"I am amazed. How did you find him so quickly?"

"I went to your hotel, Maestro, and found your carriage driver and asked him to convey me to the place where the stranger departed your company. At the nearest wineshop I asked after Zimmer, for if a man is to persist in life, he must drink wine and pay for that if for nothing else. This was not a task requiring the ingenuity of a Galileo, and I dare to hope that when you have a more complex problem you will exercise my wits more thoroughly."

"You say that you spoke to him."

"In his own dingy rooms and in the presence of a dreadful old harridan named Mme. Holzer, one who styles herself his landlady."

"Why did he not keep his appointment with me?"

"He could not. He has taken a turn for the worse. He lies in bed, pale and weak and wasting away. I shall be much surprised if he rises from this bed again."

"Is death so near?"

"Rudolf Zimmer is convinced that Death sits in a chair in his own room. But he is less concerned about death, Maestro, than about breaking his appointment with you."

"But if he is so terribly ill. . . ?"

"He is nevertheless most anxious to see you. He has a little packet of materials to give you and he is determined to tell his story, as he had promised."

"To tell his story?"

"What he said, *cher maître,* was that in telling you his story he would be placing the coda on his sonatina. Can you interpret those words?"

"We must go to him," Offenbach said, "and we must take a physician with us."

"The sawboneses he will not abide. You must not mention them in his presence if you do not wish him to grow sullen and silent."

"Then we must persuade him to show better judgment. Let me conclude a few details here and we will go immediately."

But then, with one vexation and another, it was an hour before Offenbach could disengage himself, and he was in no peaceful temper. Cherubino had a carriage standing by and the two of them got in and drove off. As they went along, Offenbach tried to calm himself.

The scene was just as Cherubino had depicted. In a little low room on the third floor Zimmer lay in a narrow bed pushed against the wall. Mme. Holzer sat in a sagging chair in the corner, as unfeeling and inexpressive as a tumbril, watching the last hours of her tenant with dull eyes. She was dressed in a huge snuff-colored dress and a grease-spotted apron and she munched continually upon cinnamon pastilles. The pungency of her sweetened breath pervaded the room.

Cherubino leaned against the door frame, observing with lively interest. His lips were rounded and Offenbach knew that a song ran in his mind; he was whistling silently. This realization irritated the composer and he turned his attention to Zimmer.

It was plain to see the man was dying. He was weak and distant, but his voice was strong and he was bent on telling his story as clearly and efficiently as possible, and without the least trace of self-pity.

Offenbach perched precariously on the edge of the bed. Zimmer first asked him to pick up a brown paper parcel that was lying on the floor and to open it.

When he did, he found a gold locket containing a lock of silver-blond hair, a sapphire ring, a faded love letter composed in a young and well-bred feminine hand, and the piano sheets of an old-fashioned waltz dedicated to "Rosalie."

He was not in the least surprised to discover that the first eight bars of this music comprised the soulful muse song his sisters had sung to him in childhood, the music that had haunted his life and in some sense had refashioned it. Nor was he surprised to find that Zimmer was the composer.

"We were very happy, my Rosalie and I," Zimmer said, "but, as you know, Maestro, the philosophers tell us that happiness is only an illusion. Yet she was beautiful, angelic, too beautiful for this world. Her father was opposed to our marriage. I am a musician; that single fact was enough for him. But her mother was our ally. I employed every strata- gem and made every kind of promise and was at last trium- phant. The day was set; the arrangements were completed. Neither of us could think of anything but our wedding day nor foresee any future but a long, delightful one of kisses and music and children."

"She must have been a wonderful young lady," Offen- bach said.

"She was perfect." Zimmer gripped the composer's left hand with a startling power. "That is no exaggeration of the lover, only a fact. She was perfect, and that is why she was taken away. Nothing perfect is allowed to abide upon the earth. A brief glimpse only, and it is snatched from us."

"Yes."

"But I do not see how you can agree with me," Zimmer said. His voice was quite harsh now with the force of his emotions. "You who have everything you desire, you who have met with the richest success. There is nothing lacking to you."

"I am a lucky man, as well I understand. Yet I have met with disappointments, too. One of them is here." Offen- bach touched the parcel open on his knees.

"What is that?"

"I would have given a great deal to have written this song, 'To Rosalie.' I cannot begin to say what it has meant to me. This song at least is a perfect thing abiding on the earth."

"You would not want to pay the cost of writing it. Rosa- lie died on the evening before our wedding day. They said her heart was weak in a way no one could suspect and that the excitement of the impending ceremony was too much for her. Two years later I wrote this waltz in her memory. I had never written music before and I have written none since."

"Even as a single work, and a small one, it shows true genius."

"Maestro, it does not. It shows the spirit of a very ordinary man in agony. In every life there must be some moment of such sorrow that it lifts our capacities to their uttermost."

"Permit me to believe," Offenbach said, "that you have a grand undeveloped talent."

Zimmer gave him a stare of frightening intensity. "Believe *me*. For another song like this one to be written, another Rosalie would have to die."

"Surely not," he exclaimed. "I'm certain I do not comprehend what you mean." Offenbach's head began to throb; the odor of Mme. Holzer's cinnamon breath was suffocating.

"I say only that you imperfectly understand the sources of your art," Zimmer said. His voice had sunk to a hoarse whisper. "In its heart your music is not so light and gay and carefree as you take pains to make it sound. In its heart yours is a sad music indeed."

"I think you may be correct," he said, "but is this not true of all music?"

Zimmer frowned. He raised himself on his elbows. "You will never understand me. Never." His rush of feeling subsided now and he lay back, staring at the ceiling. "You may go away now," he said in a voice weakened and tremulous. "You have the locket, the waltz, the sapphire ring that was to be her wedding-night gift. You have heard my story, all of it that matters. The part you play in my life is concluded, though I think that poor Rudolf shall linger on in yours."

"I will send for a doctor. No matter how much you protest."

"Will you then give me the trouble of sending him away? I am very tired. I want to rest. I want you to leave and to take with you what remains of my life."

"I will stay with you here."

"I could not bear for you to see me die. Surely I need no final humiliation heaped upon me. Please go. Go now."

Offenbach did as he was told. He gathered the locket, the letter, the ring, and the waltz into the square of brown paper and retied the string. When he turned, he found Cherubino in the act of giving Mme. Holzer a knowing wink. And as he brushed by the dirty brown old woman, he heard her mutter in an exhalation of cinnamon breath, "Up to his little tricks again."

For a week he worked at the theater with a fine conscientiousness, rehearsing the orchestra and overseeing every detail of production and publicity. He tried to put the fate of Zimmer out of his mind, but could not. On Thursday Cherubino appeared in the dressing room to tell him that Rudolf Zimmer had died peacefully, without the name of Rosalie or any other upon his lips. Cherubino delivered this information cheerfully and casually, as if he was reporting no more than a new infatuation of the principal soprano, and Offenbach was so angry with his manner that he had to stifle an impulse to strike him. Instead, he reached into his pocket and gave him two gold coins. He was convinced that if he actually had struck Cherubino, he would leave only a bright smear of damp powder, the mortal remains of a butterfly.

That night Offenbach lay in bed, suspended in the wandering state of mind that occurs before sleep. As always, there came to him the wordless singing of his sisters, the waltz of Rudolf Zimmer. But now the odor of cinnamon pastilles accompanied the sound, and the lumpish shape of Mme. Holzer was present.

He jerked awake and sat up. He peered into the darkness of his room and wished for forgetfulness.

When he lay down again, he forced himself to think of

a different sort of music, any music that differed strongly in character from the plaintive waltz. There occurred to him then the strains of his own cancan from *La Vie parisienne*, noisy and exuberant.

He remembered the origin of the dance. Before he had given it its present legitimate eminence, it had been a raw music of the streets, and when the whores and factory girls danced it, they took pains to wear no culottes. They raised their skirts high and twinkled their bare bottoms at the stars that twinkle so coolly down upon our planet. It was gay and defiant and full of a bitter courage. The memory of the cancan soothed Offenbach as it ebbed away in his mind, to be replaced, note by note, with Zimmer's waltz as he drifted to sleep, the slow voices rolling over him forever the scent of cinnamon.

WEIRD TALES

 The visionary poet Hart Crane and the equally visionary horror-story writer H. P. Lovecraft met four times. The first time was in Cleveland on August 19, 1922, in the apartment of a mutual acquaintance, the mincing poetaster Samuel Loveman.

It was an awkward encounter. Loveman and four of his idle friends had departed around eleven o'clock to go in search of a late supper. Lovecraft was sitting in an armchair under the lamp, a calico kitten asleep in his lap. He declined the invitation to accompany the others because he would not disturb the kitten; cats comprised another of his numerous manias. Shortly before midnight Crane blundered into the room. He was enjoying this night one of his regular fits of debauchery and was quite drunk. "'Lo," he said. "I'm Crane. Where's Sam?" He took no notice of Lovecraft's puzzled stare, but raked a half dozen volumes of French poetry from the sofa, lay down, and passed out.

Lovecraft was quite put off, though the poet's quick slide

to oblivion had spared him a dilemma. He would have had to rise in order to present himself, and thus awaken the cat. Lovecraft insisted upon precise formality of address; it was part of his pose as an eighteenth-century esquire sadly comported into the Jazz Age. He was a fanatic teetotaler, and Crane's stuporous condition filled him with disgust.

When Loveman and two companions returned a half hour later, the cat had awakened and Lovecraft set it gently on the floor, rose, and walked to the door. He paused and pointed a finger at Crane, at the ungainly form overpowered with gin and rumpled by the attentions of sailors. "Samuel," he said to Loveman, "your friend is a *degenerate.*"

The effect of this melodramatic sentence was marred by the quality of Lovecraft's voice, a tremulous squeak. Loveman giggled. "Then I'm a degenerate, too, Howard," he said. "Maybe we all are. Maybe that's why no one takes us seriously."

Lovecraft's reply was a toss of his unhandsome head. He closed the door and walked out into the night, walked the seventeen blocks to the YMCA, to his cheerless room and narrow bed. He undressed and, after carefully laying his pants between the mattress and springs for pressing, fell asleep and began to dream his familiar dreams of vertiginous geometries and cyclopean half gods, vivid dreams that would have been anyone else's sweat-drenched nightmares.

After two days Lovecraft and Crane met again and attended a chamber-music concert. Crane was sober then and Lovecraft was quite charmed by his company.

It was an odd group of literary figures, these poets and fiction writers and amateur scholars stranded like survivors of a shipwreck on what they considered the hostile strand of American philistinism. They were not really congenial in temperament or purpose, but they all shared a common interest in newly discovered, newly reconstructed mythologies. They felt need to posit in history powerful but invisible alien forces that had made contemporary civilization such an inhumane shambles. This sort of notion may have been an index to acute loneliness.

Lovecraft's mythos is the most widely known. In a series of fictions soon to appear in the venerated pulp magazine *Weird Tales,* he told of several eras of prehistory when mankind vied with monstrous races of creatures with extraordinary powers for a foothold upon the earth. Man's present dominance was accidentally and precariously achieved; those alien beings were beginning to rearise from their dormancy. Lovecraft described a cosmos that threw dark Lucretian doubt on the proposition ''that such things as organic life, good and evil, love and hate, and all such local attributes of a negligible and temporary race called mankind, have any existence at all.''

Hart Crane's mythology was not systematic; in fact, it was hardly articulate. His sensibility was such that he was unnerved in his brushes with the ancient presences he detected, and he could not write or think clearly about them. But his old friends were interested to note in his later poems the occurrence of such lines as, ''Couched on bloody basins, floating bones/ Of a dismounted people. . . .'' Crane believed that Poe had gained best knowledge of the Elder Dominations and so paired him with Whitman in *The Bridge* as a primary avatar of American consciousness.

The most thorough and deliberate of these mythologers was Sterling Croydon, who might have stepped from the pages of one of Lovecraft's stories. He was such a recluse that not even Samuel Loveman saw him more than once or twice a month, though he occupied an apartment in the same building with Loveman, on the floor above. Croydon rarely ventured from his rooms; all those volumes of mathematics, physics, anthropology, and poetry were delivered to his door, and he prepared his scant meals with spirit lamp and a portable gas stove. He was gracious enough to allow occasional visitors, never more than two at a time, and Loveman would spend an evening now and then listening to Croydon elaborate his own system of frightening mythologies. He had been excited to learn that Lovecraft was coming to visit in Cleveland, abandoning for a week his beloved Providence, Rhode Island, and spoke of a strong desire to meet the writer. But when Lovecraft arrived, Croydon withdrew, fearing, no doubt, that to meet the inheritor of Poe's mantle would prove too great a strain for his nerves.

He didn't appear a nervous or high-strung person, but rather—like Lovecraft—a formal gentleman and the soul of composure. He was fastidious and kept himself neatly dressed in dark wool. He imagined that he was painfully photosensitive and ordinarily resorted to dark glasses. His complexion was pale and often flushed, his frame slender almost to the point of emaciation, his gestures quick but calculated. Yet there was a dreamy grandeur about him and when he held forth on various points of Boolean algebra or primitive religion, Loveman felt that he was in the presence of strong intellect and refined character, however neurasthenic.

It was Croydon's contention that his colleagues had but scratched the surface of the problem. He had read Tylor, Sir James Frazer, Leo Frobenius and had traced their sources; he knew thoroughly the more radical attempts of Lovecraft, Clark Ashton Smith, Henry Kuttner, Frank Belknap Long, and the others, but considered that they had done no more than dredge up scraps and splinters. He was convinced that one of Lovecraft's principal sources, the *Pnakotic Manuscripts*, was spurious, and that his descriptions of such cruel gods as Nyarlathotep and Yog-Sothoth were biased and vitiated by sensationalism and overwrought prose style.

He did not claim, of course, to know the whole truth. But he did know that Riemann's concept of elliptical geometry was indispensable to a correct theory and that the magnetic fluxions of the South Pole were important in a way no one had thought of. He had been eager to apprise

Lovecraft of these ideas and of others, but at the last hour his shyness overcame him. Or maybe he had come to doubt the writer's seriousness.

We are forced to speculate about the outcome of this meeting that never took place; it might well have been of great aid to us, bringing to public notice Croydon's more comprehensive theories and engendering in Lovecraft a deeper sense of responsibility.

The one result we know, however, is that Croydon's life became even more reclusive than before. He almost never saw Loveman and his companions anymore, and no one was admitted now to his rooms. The single exception to this general exclusion was Hart Crane. Croydon thought that he saw qualities and capabilities in Crane lacking in his coarser-grained friends, and he would receive the poet anytime of the day or night. Drinking himself only a little wine, blackberry or elderberry, he kept a supply of gin for Crane, who never arrived sober and who would not stay unless there was something to drink.

So it was to Crane that Croydon poured out all his certainties, theories, and wild surmises. Almost all of it would have made no sense to Crane and would be distorted by his fever for poetry and disfigured by alcoholic forgetfulness. Yet he was impressed by this anomalous scholar, and bits and pieces of those midnight disquisitions lodged in his mind. Perhaps Croydon's talk impressed him in a way it might not have done if he had been sober. The poet was interested in pre-Columbian history, he had always had a yearning to travel in Mexico, and he was particularly taken with Croydon's notion that the Toltec, Mayan, and finally the Aztec religions were shadowy reflections of historical events that took place when mankind inhabited the Antarctic, when that region was steamy carboniferous forest. Those jaguar gods and feathered serpents that ornamented the temples had become highly stylized and symbolic, Croydon said, but long, long ago, when man and dinosaur and other less definable races coexisted at the bottom of the world, the first of these carvings and paintings had been attempts simply to represent literal appearance. Those creatures, and many others of unproducible aspect, had lived among us. Or rather, we had lived among them, as animal labor supply and as food source.

Crane discounted most of Croydon's notions. He did not believe, for example, that dinosaurs could have been intelligent warm-blooded creatures who had attempted to dislodge the alien gods who ruled among them. He did not believe the dinosaurs had died because their adversaries had infected them with an artificial bacterium that had spread like wildfire, wiping out every major saurian species in three generations. But he was fascinated by Croydon's accounts of tribal religions in South and Central America, caught up by the exotic imagery and the descriptions of ritual. Croydon was especially excited by an obscure tribe inhabiting the reaches of the upper Amazon who worshiped a panoply of gods they called collectively Dzhaimbú. Or perhaps they worshiped but one god who could take different shapes. Much was unclear. But it was clear that Croydon regarded Dzhaimbú as the most anciently rooted of religions, in a direct descent from mankind's prehistoric Antarctic experiences.

Crane was impressed, too, by another of Croydon's ideas. This scholar disagreed vehemently with Darwin's charming theory that man had learned speech by imitating the mating calls of birds. Not so, said Croydon; man was originally a vocally taciturn animal like the horse and the gorilla, and, like horse and gorilla, uttered few sounds except under duress of extreme pain or terror. But these sounds they learned to voice quite regularly when Dzhaimbú inflicted upon them unspeakable atrocities, practices that Croydon could not think of without shuddering. All human speech was merely the elaboration of an original shriek of terror.

"'S a shame, Sterling," Crane said, "that you can't board a ship and go down to the jungle and investigate. I bet you'd turn up some interesting stuff."

Croydon smiled. "Oh, I wouldn't bother with the jungle. I'd go to the Antarctic and look for direct archaeological evidence."

Crane took another swallow from his tumbler of neat gin. His eyes were slightly unfocused and his face was flushed and his neck red in the soft open collar. "Shame you can't go to the South Pole then, if that's where you want to go."

"No, I shouldn't make a very able sailor, I think," Croydon said. "But, after all, there are other ways to travel than by crawling over the globe like a termite."

And now he launched into a description of what he called spatial emplacement, by which means a man sitting in his room might visit any part of the earth. All that was required was delicate manipulation of complex and tenuous mathematical formulae, prediction of solar winds, polar magnetic fluxions, cosmic-ray vectors, and so forth. He began to pour out a rubble of numbers and Greek letters, all of which Crane disregarded, suspecting that they'd struck now upon the richest vein of his friend's lunacy. Croydon's idea seemed to be that every geographical location in the universe could be imagined as being located on the surface of its individual sphere, and that the problem was simply to turn these spheres until the desired points matched and touched. Touched, but did not conjoin; there would be disaster if they conjoined. The worst complication was that these mathematical spheres, once freed from Euclidean space, were also free in time. One might arrive to inspect Antarctica at the time he wished, which would be pleasant indeed; or he might arrive in the future, uncountable millenia from now. And that would be dangerous as well as inconvenient.

But all this murmur of number and mathematical theory had lulled Crane. He was asleep in the club chair. Croydon woke him gently and suggested that he might like to go home.

"Yeah, maybe I better," Crane said. He scratched his

head, disheveling again his spiky hair. "But say, Sterling, I don't know about the travel by arithmetic. Better to get a berth on a ship and sail around and see the birds wheel overhead and the slow islands passing." The thought struck his enthusiasm. "That's what we'll do one of these days. We'll get on a ship and go explore these jungles."

"Good night, Hart," Croydon said.

This impulsive voyage was never to take place, of course. Crane's poetry had begun to attract important critical notice, and he soon moved to New York to further his melancholy but luminous literary career.

Croydon remained behind to pursue his researches ever more intensively. He was quite lost sight of to the world. Loveman would occasionally stop by but was not admitted.

It was on one of these infrequent visits that he felt a strangeness. The hall leading to Croydon's room was chilly and the air around the door very cold indeed. And the door was sweating cold water, had begun to collect ice around the edges. The brass nameplate was covered with hard frost, obliterating Croydon's name.

Loveman knocked and knocked again and heard no sound within but a low inhuman moan. He tried the icy knob, which finally turned, but could not force the door inward. He braced his feet, set his shoulder against the door, and strained, but was able to get it open only for the space of an inch or two. The noise increased—it was the howling of wind—and a blast of rumbling air swept over him and he saw in that small space only an area of white, a patch of snow. Then the wind thumped the door shut.

Loveman was at a loss. None of his usual friends was nearby to aid him, and he would not call upon others. He belonged to a circle in which there were many secrets they did not wish the larger world to know. He returned to his rooms on the lower floor, dressed himself in a winter woolen jacket and scarf and toboggan. After a brief search he found his gloves. He took a heavy ornamental brass

poker from the hearth and returned to Croydon's door.
This time he set himself firmly and, when he had effected
a slight opening, thrust the poker into the space and lev-
ered it back. The poker began to bend with the strain and
he could feel the coldness of it through his gloves. Then
the wind caught the edge of the door and flung it back
suddenly and Loveman found himself staring into a snowy
plain swept over by fierce Antarctic wind.

It was all very puzzling. Loveman could see into this
windstorm and feel some force of the wind and cold, but
he knew that what he felt was small indeed as compared
to the fury of the weather into which he could see. Nor
could he advance physically into this landscape. He could
march forward, pushing against the wind, he could feel
himself going forward, but he did not advance so much as
an inch into that uproar of ice and snow.

It is in another space, he thought, but very, very close to
my own.

He could see into it but he could not travel there. In fact,
with the wild curtains of snow blowing he could see little,
but what he could see was terrible enough.

There, seemingly not twenty feet from him, sat Croydon
at his desk. The scholar was wearing only his burgundy
velvet dressing gown and gray flannel trousers and bedroom slippers. The habitual dark glasses concealed his eyes,
but the rest of his face was drawn into a tortured grimace.

Of course Loveman shouted out *"Croydon! Croydon!"*
knowing it was useless.

He could not tell whether his friend was still alive. He
did not think that he could be. Certainly if he was in the
same space as this Antarctic temperature, he must have
died a quick but painful death. Perhaps he was not in that
space but in a space like Loveman's own, touching but not
conjoining this polar location. Yet the Antarctic space inter-
vened between them, an impassable barrier.

He wished now that he had paid more attention when
Croydon had outlined his mathematical ideas. But Love-

man, like Crane, had no talent for, no patience with, number. He could never have understood. And now those pages of painstaking calculation had blown away, stiff as steel blades, over the blue ice sheets.

He thought that if he could not walk forward then he might crawl, but when he went to his knees he found himself suspended a couple of feet above the plane of the floor. Something was wrong with the space he was in. He stood dizzily and stepped down to the floor again, and the descent was as hard a struggle as climbing an Alpine precipice.

There was no way to get to Croydon, and he wondered whether it would be possible to heave a rope to him—if he could find a rope.

It was impossible. The scholar had begun to recede in space, growing smaller and more distant, as if caught in the wrong end of a telescope. And the polar wind began to effect a bad transformation. The dressing gown was ripped from Croydon's body and he was blackening like a gardenia thrown into a fire. His skin and the layers of his flesh began to curl up and peel away, petal by petal. A savage gust tore off his scalp and the blood that welled there froze immediately, a skullcap of onyx. Soon he would be only a skeleton, tumbled knob and joint over the driving snow, but Loveman was spared the spectacle. The frozen figure receded more quickly and a swirl of ice grains blotted away the vision. Croydon was gone.

Loveman made his way into the hall, walking backward. His mouth was dully open and he found that he was sweating and that the sweat had begun to ice his clothing.

There came a crash as of thunder, the smell of ozone, and the Antarctic scene disappeared from the room and there was nothing there. Literally, nothing: no furniture, no walls, no floor. The door with Croydon's nameplate hung over a blue featureless abyss. There was nothing, no real space at all.

Loveman gathered his courage, reached in, and pulled

the door closed. He went quietly down the hall, determined
to get back into his own room before others showed up.
He did not want to answer questions; he did not want anyone to know what he knew. He wanted to go to his room
and sit down and think alone and reaffirm his sanity.
The disappearance of Croydon and of that part of the
apartment building caused some little public stir. The recluse had no relatives, but scientists were interested, as well
as the police. Loveman avoided as best he could any official
notice, and in a few months the event, being unexplain-
able, was largely forgotten.

But the occurrence was not forgotten by the circle of Loveman's friends. For them it was a matter of great concern.
They feared that Croydon's experiment had called attention
to themselves. Would not those alien presences whose histories they had been studiously examining now turn their
regard toward Cleveland? Had he not disturbed the web of
space-time as a fly disturbs a spiderweb? It was true that
they were indifferent to mankind, to species and individual
alike. But there were some researchers who thought, as
Lovecraft did, that the ancient race was planning a regener-
ation of its destiny and would act to keep its existence secret until the moment was ripe. The powers of these beings
was immense; they could crush and destroy when and
where they pleased, as casually as a man crushes out a cigarette in an ashtray.

It was actually at this early juncture that everything began
to come apart. Though the pursuit among the seers and
poets was leisurely by human standards, it was relentless.
Lovecraft died in 1937, in painful loneliness. The official
medical report listed the cause as intestinal cancer, but the
little group of investigators was accustomed to greeting all
such reports with deep skepticism. Hart Crane's more famous death had taken place five years earlier, the celebrated leap into the sea.

The men had since met twice again, during the period of what Lovecraft called his "New York exile." He was a little shocked at the changes in Crane's physical condition. "He looks more weatherbeaten & drink-puffed than he did in the past," Lovecraft wrote to his aunt, "tragically drink-riddled but now eminent." He predicted that Crane would find it difficult to write another major work. "After about three hours of acute & intelligent argument poor Crane left—to hunt up a new supply of whiskey & banish reality for the rest of the night!"

Lovecraft records this encounter as taking place May 24, 1930. They were not alone and had no opportunity to talk privately, so that Crane would not have told the other what he had learned of the circumstances of Croydon's death. He could not apprise Lovecraft that he alone was inheritor to Croydon's secret knowledge and that his identity must necessarily be known to that being, or series of beings, Dzhaimbú. He spoke of leaving New York and moving to Charleston, but Lovecraft did not pick up the hint, merely agreeing that such a move might be beneficial. Perhaps Crane's gallantry prevented his placing the other in danger.

Another interpretation is possible. We may guess that Crane did indeed communicate some of his information to the horror-story writer. It is just at this period that Lovecraft's mythos began to take its more coherent and credible shape in such works as "The Shadow Over Innsmouth" and "The Dreams in the Witch House." Certainly both Lovecraft and Loveman remarked that Crane now lived in a state of haunted terror, wild and frightful, dependent upon alcohol to keep his fear manageable. Crane must have known that he was being pursued—the signs were unmistakable—and decided to face the terror on its own grounds. For this reason he politicked to get the Guggenheim grant that would take him to Mexico.

But it was too late. Alcohol had disordered his nervous system; his strength was gone. On the voyage to Mexico he met the celebrated bacteriologist Dr. Hans Zinsser and imagined that he was an agent of Dzhaimbú sent to infect humanity by means of typhus-ridden rats. Zinsser's motives in dumping infected rats into the harbor at Havana remain unknown, but it is hardly probable that Crane's suspicions were correct.

In Mexico the poet's behavior was uncontrolled and incomprehensible, a series of shocking and violent incidents that landed him often in jail and caused his friends to distrust any sentence he uttered. His decision to meet the terror face-to-face was disastrous; he could not stand up under the strain. No man could. And his further decision to keep his knowledge and theories secret so as not to endanger others was a worse disaster.

In the end, he fled, unable to face the prospect of coming close to the source of the horror. The voyage home began with dreams and visions so terrifying that he could not bear to close his eyes and so stayed awake, drinking continuously. Embarrassing episodes followed of which he was numbly aware but past caring about. On April 27, 1932, Hart Crane jumped from the railing of the *Orizaba*. The sea received him and the immense serpentine manifestation of Dzhaimbú, which had been following in the unseen depths the wake of the vessel, devoured him.

This fabulous shadow only the sea keeps.

It is inevitable that we read these sad histories as we do, as a catalogue of missed opportunities and broken communications. A present generation self-righteously decries the errors of its forefathers. But it is unlikely that any human effort would have changed the course of events. There still would have come about the reawakening of Dzhaimbú and the other worse gods, under whose charnel dominion we now suffer and despair.

THE SOMEWHERE DOORS

 No true light yet showed in the window, but he could feel the dawn coming on, the softness of it brushing his neck hair like a whisper, and heard the stir of trees outside the screen of his open window. He sat staring at the paper before him, the Blue Horse page he had so painstakingly covered with his light slant strokes, and held his pen poised above it, ready to write the final line of his story.

Here was his keenest pleasure, writing down at last the sentence he had aimed at from the beginning. It was like drawing the line beneath a column of numbers and setting in the sum, a feeling not only of winding up but of full completion. He waited, savoring the moment, then inscribed the words: "Lixor looked at the lights in the sky and wondered if one of them would begin to move toward him." And then, to prolong his satisfaction, he printed THE END below in tall, graceful capitals embellished with curls of flourish. Reverting to his careful script, he put down also his name: *Arthur Strakl, Cherry Cove, North Carolina, September 12, 1936.*

When he looked at his handiwork, his name seemed
strange to him, out of place on this page full of exotic sights
and notions, as homely alien as a worn tin thimble in a
jeweler's fancy display case. So he set about inking the
postscript out, producing a shiny black rectangle where
each word had stood. The page looked better, he thought,
without this reminder of our world of familiar impressions
and of a dispiriting time in a place that was all too local.
Anyhow, he would see his name enough times when "The
Marooned Aldebaran" was published.

If it was published.

His luck was not good. Only about three of ten of the
stories that he wrote ever saw print, and then in so mutilated a fashion, so mangled by editorial obtuseness, that he
felt a sad weariness when they did appear.

He went to his one bookcase and took up a copy of a
recent *Astounding Stories* from an unread stack of similar
pulp magazines. It was the August issue, and commenced
The Incredible Invasion, a serial novel by Murray Leinster.
Names familiar to habitués of this kind of literature were
displayed: Weinbaum, Fearn, Schachner, Gallun, and Will-
iamson. The cover illustration showed grim hominoids in
gleaming gray armor battling among themselves and menacing a brace of plucky young ladies in dapper short skirts.
He supposed the armored men to be the Incredible Invad-
ers. Arthur did not read invasion stories; he could not
imagine that Earth, unfashionable and located far from its
galactic center, would be a desirable prize.

We are, he reflected, a bunch of hicks. Why would anyone bother?

Opening the magazine, he flipped past the ads for self-
education and self-medication, but his attention was drawn
to the announcement for a new character pulp, *The Whisperer.* "The Whisperer!—NOT a Chinaman!—NOT a modern Robin Hood!—NOT a myth or a ghost!—But—HE
IS———a good two-fisted, hard-hitting AMERICAN cop
who gets his man!''

Arthur sighed, thinking how he could never write a story about The Whisperer, how in fact he probably could never bring himself to read one. He had tried to write some of those stories about two-fisted cops, two-fisted cowboys, two-fisted orphans of the jungle male and female, but that talent was not in him—nor for flying aces, nor scientific detectives, nor steel-armed quarterbacks or boxers. Again it was a question of belief. He did not believe that human beings came from so predictable a toy box and he could not engage himself in heroic fantasies. To him those daydreams lacked imagination and verged upon braggartry. But he did not wish to condemn. Hard times now, and writers needed to stock groceries, and readers wished to enjoy the brief glimpses of triumph the pulp stories afforded.

But his own stories were not fashioned in that mode. He could write only these melancholy twilight visions of things distant in time and space, stories that seemed not entirely his, but gifts or visitations from a source at which he could not guess. His most difficult task was to find words for them; he was a shy man, naturally taciturn, and he considered himself unhandy with language. But when the stories came to him, the impulse to write them down was too strong to resist. The stories compelled him to write, to struggle with phrases in a way that felt incongruous to his personality. And so he wrote, stealing the hours from his bed, the strength from his body. Each stroke of the pen, every noun and comma and period, brought him closer to the beautiful release that he always felt, as he did now, upon completion of a tale.

That was the main thing, to finish, to tell the stories through to the end. He got not much money for them and what he received was always late in arriving, and little acclaim came his way, for the readers who wrote to the letter columns preferred the loud, brawny stories of superscience, with their whirling rays and burning cities, colliding suns and flaming rocket ships, to his delicate accounts of loneliness under the stars, his elegies for dying worlds and soul-

ful perishing species. Of course, his stories as they appeared
were mutilated so that readers could not form fair opinions
about them, but Arthur suspected that even if they were
published just as they came in their final drafts from his
typewriter, with every nuance and adverb complete, readers still would prefer the yarns about genius engineers and
iron-thewed swordsmen.

He replaced the magazine on top of the stack and paced
the narrow strip of floor between his desk and the foot of
his lumpy bed. He was too elated to sleep and, anyway,
the night was nearly gone. A dim gray began to show in
the window. He would go to his job at the Red Man Café
red-eyed and nervous and in the afternoon a dull lassitude
would creep over him and he would drink cup after cup of
acid coffee until closing time. He was "chief cook and bottle washer," as the owner, Farley Redmon, called him, and
his hours were long and ill paid. But he earned his food
and his rent for this little outbuilding that was formerly a
tool shed—and he had a job and in this year of Our Lord
1936, he was grateful for it.

He would be grateful to light down anywhere he could
find in order to write these stories that gave him no peace.

Arthur decided to walk out. The excitement of composition was still warm in him and the hour was inviting, cool
and quiet. He pulled on his thinning blue wool sweater and
peered out his window and, seeing no lights in any of the
settlement windows, departed his room, taking care to turn
off the little desk lamp with its green cardboard shade.

Cherry Cove was quiet, almost silent: no dogs barking,
no radios in kitchens reporting farm prices, no clatter of
breakfast cutlery. Everyone snug and warm and dreaming
and, as he walked along the broad gravel road that led east,
Arthur wondered whether any of their dreams might be as
strange as the one he had just set down, in which the last
survivor of a race of orchidaceous philosophers journeyed
to the moon of its planet in order to send a signal to the
cosmos, a message telling them that though the Kronori

had died all but Lixor, he had one valuable secret to share with every other species everywhere.

Arthur smiled, assuring himself that the dreams of his neighbors would be stranger and more exciting and more urgent than his little tale. Then he set out at an easy walking pace for the Little Tennessee River two miles distant, the river that ran counter to all the others.

He was headed toward the peeling iron bridge. He had no particular purpose in mind, drawn only by that obscure impulse that leads us to the sound of running water as a source of comfort and refreshment. When he stood there at the railing, listening to the water twenty feet below rush away over the rocks—going the wrong way, for the Little Tennessee is a backwards river—his anxieties fell quiet and the utter lack of hope that characterized his days took on the aspect of courage rather than of fear. Arthur Strakl often felt that he stood on the abrupt edge of an ebony abyss, and that if he fell he would fall without crying out, without making a sound, and that no one on earth would remark his passing or remember that he had sojourned here. These considerations sometimes made him gloomy; at other times they strengthened his resolve, and did so now, with the completion of "The Marooned Aldebaran" fresh in his mind. He listened to the water and smelled its clean smell and watched where the river drew away into the forest of firs and oaks. On his right-hand side, just at the bridgehead, was a stand of slender trees with flowers beneath, and he glanced at it without really seeing it.

Then he became aware that he was not alone on the bridge. A woman stood beside him. He had not heard her approach, but he was not startled; her aspect was calm and easy. He was surprised to see that she was dressed in a white silk party frock with a wide square collar. She wore white pumps of patent leather and her dark hair was tied back with a broad ribbon of shiny white silk.

She was a beautiful woman, and when she spoke, it was

with a quiet musical accent that was stranger than any other he had ever heard. "Are you Arthur Strakl?" she asked.

"Yes ma'am," he said, though she was not his elder. She looked rather younger than Arthur's thirty-five years.

"I'm glad," she said, and said no more for such a long moment that he began to think the conversation had ended. Then she added, "To meet you. I'm glad to meet you."

"I'm glad to meet you, too. You don't live in Cherry Cove, do you?"

"No," she said. "I've come a long way to find you."

"Me?" He laughed. "Well now, that's a little hard to believe."

"Why is it hard to believe?"

Arthur noted that she spoke slowly and hesitantly, as if these words were foreign to her. "There's no good reason for anyone to look for me. I don't have a family or any close friends. No one knows who I am."

"Are you not Arthur Strakl, the author?"

"I write a few odd stories. I never thought of calling myself an author."

"But didn't you write 'In the Titanic Deeps,' the story about sea dwellers in another galaxy?"

"Yes. My title was 'Blind Oceans,' but they changed it. That one was about the great worms that lived on the bottom of an ocean. They were suffering because they had the power to foresee centuries into the future and saw that nothing would change, that their destiny was fixed. Then one of their mathematicians devised a theory that admitted the possibility of the end of time, and this idea brought solace to them."

"And then what happened?"

"Nothing," he said. "That was it. . . . Well, their music changed."

She turned upon him a superbly friendly smile. Dawn brightened over the river below them. "Yes," she said. "Their music changed."

"I'm amazed," he said. "You can't imagine. This is the first time I ever met somebody who has read one of my stories."

"Oh, I've read many of your stories. I remember them all."

"Well, I actually haven't published all that many."

"I remember your story about the beings you called 'kindlers.' They were incandescent blue nervous systems that lived on the surface of a faraway sun. I remember the planet you called Zephlar, where the wind streaming over a continent of telepathic grasses produced an unending silent musical fugue. I remember your city Alphega, which was an enormous machine that was writing a book; each word of the book was a living human citizen. I remember your story about the language you named Spranza, which communicated so efficiently that listeners experienced directly the objects and actions it spoke of. And the sentient river Luvulio that had become a religious zealot, and the single amber eye named Ull, which lay in a primordial sea waiting for the remainder of its organism to evolve, and the parasite that reproduced itself by causing allergies in its hosts. At the magnetic pole of a tropical planet grew a tree whose leaves were mirrors; there was a world where humanlike people communicated by differences in skin temperature. There was a plague virus that heightened the sense of taste to painful degree."

"Good Lord," Arthur said.

"So you see," she said sweetly, "I have read your stories. They have afforded me"—she paused, as if waiting for the correct phrase to present itself—"a fine pleasure. Many fine pleasures."

"Thank you for saying so," Arthur said. "But I didn't write all those stories. Somebody else must have written about the religious river and the alphabet city. And none of the magazines would take my story about the telepathic grasses. I don't see how you could have heard about that one."

"You have more admirers than you're aware of," she said. She smiled and turned away to watch the early light smear tree shadows on the river surface. "Sometimes the editors talk about your stories even when they don't buy them. Sometimes they want to buy them and are afraid to. But word gets around."

"Well, you obviously know a great deal about this," he said. "What do you do for a living? I mean, are you a literary agent?"

"I'm a representative for a group of people who are interested in new ideas," she said. "They have great faith in the power of ideas to make the future better for everyone."

"Who are they?"

She turned to meet his gaze directly. Her brown eyes were serious. "They prefer to remain anonymous."

"Are they Communists then?" he asked. "I met a Communist once who talked like that, sort of."

She laughed lightly. "I don't think they belong to any recognizable political group. . . . To tell the truth, I don't know all that much about them. They just pay me to deliver messages to people they think are important to their way of looking at things."

"And I'm important to them?"

"Oh yes," she said, and there was no mistaking the sincerity of her reply. "Extremely important. They're very pleased to discover you. That's why they sent me to trace you down."

"How did you find out where I live?"

"It wasn't hard. You are a publishing author, after all." She laughed again, and the light sound reminded Arthur of a child's laughter.

He found himself smiling. "Only a few people know about that."

"But it's not how many," she said. "It's who they are."

"And these are important people?"

"I don't know anything about them," she said, "but they seem to have decided that they're important."

"So now you know who I am, but I don't know who you are."

"I'm not supposed to tell my real name. I was supposed to choose any name that I took a fancy to. Do I look like a Francesca?"

"I don't know," he said. "I've never seen any Francescas."

"So this must be exciting for you." She offered her hand. "It's nice to meet you, Arthur."

He held it for a moment. "I'm pleased to meet you, too. May I ask about the way you're dressed? Or is that against the rules?"

"Oh, this," she said. "Of course. I came from a dinner party that went on till too late, so then I came straight here."

"Straight here to this bridge?"

"Yes."

Confused, he could not formulate the question he wanted to ask. "How did you get here?"

"My driver dropped me off," she said, and hurried on to add, "and the car will be returning for me very soon. So I'd better go ahead and deliver my message."

"From these unknown people?"

"Yes." She laughed again and now there was something teasing in the sound—teasing but not mocking. "Yes, my message that I don't understand from a group of people I don't know. . . . This doesn't really make sense, does it?"

"No," he said. "But I don't much care. A lot of things don't make sense to me."

"I'll bet you like it better that way."

"I do." His tone changed. "I sure do wish you lived around here. Are you married?"

She reached gently to touch his face with two fingers. "You're sweet. Truly. It's very sweet of you to say that. But I live far away and our time is short. I'd better tell you what I came to say."

"All right." He grinned. "Fire when ready."

She closed her eyes for a moment, then opened them.
"Two doors will be brought to you. Don't be afraid. These
doors open to other worlds, worlds different from our own.
Behind the blue door is a world that has no people in it.
The violet door is the entrance to a world of great cities.
You can live in either world very pleasantly, but once you
choose either door, you can never return. You will be gone
from this planet forever."

"Wait. I don't understand."

"It's no good asking me," she said. "I don't understand,
either. I can only tell you what I was told."

"Did they send a letter?" he asked. "I'd like to read it."

"It was a telephone message and the voice sounded like
it came from a long way off. I couldn't even tell if it was
a man or a woman speaking."

"Is that all then? Two doors?"

She closed her eyes once more, appearing to recollect,
then went on: "The two doors will be brought to you at
some future date. It may be soon, or it may be quite some
time from now. And things may happen so that you think
the doors never will arrive. But they will."

"Where will I find them?"

"I don't know," she said.

"All right. What else?"

"Nothing else."

"That's all?"

"As far as I can think, that's the end of the message. I
hope I haven't forgotten anything. . . . Oh, don't look so
alarmed. I'm sure I haven't."

"I honestly don't know what to make of all this."

"Neither do I," she replied, smiling her fine smile once
more. "I'm just glad I don't have to make sense of it.
—Wait. Now I remember. There was one other thing. You
must keep writing your wonderful stories. That is the most
important thing. You must keep on imagining the kinds of
things that only you can imagine."

"All right. I wish I could sell more of them, though. I
could use the money."

"I'm sorry. The person I talked to didn't say anything about that. But I'm sure you'll do well. —Oh, here comes my ride." She raised her right arm and waved.

He turned, to see that the car was at the end of the bridge, by the stand of birches there, rolling very slowly toward them, almost silent on the gravel. That was strange, and the car was strange, too, with its darkened windows and its smooth, almost featureless sedan shape and its deep oxblood color. There was something dreamlike about its appearance as it came on slowly.

When it drew abreast of them, it stopped and the passenger door opened—seemingly of its own accord—and the girl got in easily, showing neat ankles and pulling her skirt over her knees. He leaned down, trying to see the driver, but the car was in shadow on that side.

"Goodbye, Arthur," she said. Her tone was grave now and she didn't smile.

"I suppose I won't see you again."

"No," she said. "Never again."

"I hate it," he said. "I wish—"

"No. Say goodbye."

"All right. . . . Goodbye." He sighed.

And she closed the door and the strange smooth car pulled away, the sound of its motor no more than a warm hum and soon lost in the normal sounds of an autumn morning by the water: birdcalls and squirrels frolicking and the wash and gurgle of the river. He watched the car till it floated out of sight around the tall bank of the road all yellow and red with locust and sassafras bushes.

Two years passed and Arthur Strakl waited patiently. He had a serene confidence that the two doors, the doors that opened upon different Somewheres, would be brought to him. He did not know why he was so secure in his faith; he was not introspective in that particular way. The fancies that his mind produced entranced him, but the workings of his mind held no interest.

Not much changed. His employer, Farley Redmon, had undertaken to make his hut a little more comfortable, paying to have it plumbed and rewired. But he explained that he could not increase Arthur's wages and Arthur accepted the statement, his needs few. His heaviest expenses outside basic necessities were his pulp magazines and typewriter ribbons and now and again some small fees for the repair of the ancient Underwood. He was healthy and lucky.

For he kept on writing his stories, just as he had promised, and he was beginning to have a brighter success with them. He was still no great favorite with readers, but their letters now spoke of his work with intrigued bemusement rather than with irritated incomprehension. He appeared more regularly in the magazines and now and then his name would be featured on the cover, tucked away in the corner of the pictured insane laboratory where the flimsily clothed girl stared in horror at some loathsome transformation.

His better satisfaction, though, was that editors began to do less violence to his sentences. His style of writing was still hobbledehoy, he thought, but it was better left alone than improved. At least something of the intensity of his visions flamed through, even if sensual nuance was lost. The essential strangeness of the tales did not diminish. He wrote, for instance, a story based on the idea that the positions of the stars in our galaxy had been designed by the immensely powerful science of an ancient superrace as a kind of wallpaper. In another story the ghost of a dismantled robot visited its inventor and sat each night silent and reproachful at the foot of his bed. In "Black Receiver" an intelligent butterfly composed of a carbon gas picked up through its antennae the radio communications of a space fleet and thus formed a very surprising view of humankind.

So he was fairly content and hoped for better things to come, even though it was clear that the times were verging on catastrophe. Arthur was no great reader of newspapers, but no one could escape hearing about the events in Europe, and all the world was darkened by suspicion.

Arthur's own apprehensiveness deepened when he was visited by a man who claimed to be a government agent and asked whether he knew Sheila Weddell. "I don't think so," he said. "The name doesn't ring a bell."
The agent gave him a long stare. Then he said, "All right, sport. I'll have coffee."
When Arthur set the thick mug before him, the squat little man added cream and three spoons of sugar before saying, "You sure?"
"Sure of what?"
"About the woman. Sheila Weddell."
"I don't know her." He knew, however, that he didn't like this dumpy little man with his false smile that let the sneer show through and his slicked-back silver-blond hair. He had a firm impression of the fellow as one who took deep satisfaction in feeling contempt. His bored eyes and twisted mouth betrayed a jaded spirit.
"I got a picture." He reached into his inside jacket pocket and produced a crinkled photograph.
The picture, as Arthur had expected, was of the woman who called herself Francesca, and he already had decided to keep this agent—if that's what he was—at arm's length. "Pretty," he said, and handed it back.
The man laid it carefully on the Bakelite counter, then turned it around to face Arthur. "You've seen her before, haven't you? About two years ago?"
"Two years is a long time."
"It's longer inside the jailhouse than it is outside. Even in a fleabite place like this." He giggled. "What do you call it here? Cherry Cola?"
"Cherry Cove," Arthur said. "You're in Cherry Cove, North Carolina."
"And I want to know if you ain't seen this woman, Sheila Weddell, in Cherry Cove, North Carolina, about two years ago."

"You say you're some kind of an agent? I'd like to see your identification."

He drew a toothpick from an upper vest pocket and stuck it in the front of his mouth, so it bobbed up and down as he spoke. "You know, sport, I don't think you'd be asking for identification unless you were trying to hide something. I got me an idea you're hiding something."

"And I have an idea you're no government agent of any kind," Arthur said. "I have an idea you're a lawyer or a Pinkerton who is meddling in a lady's private affairs."

"I see. You kinda like her, do you? Well, let me tell you, you don't know what's going on. You don't know the least little thing. If you did, you wouldn't be calling Sheila Weddell no lady. I guess she must have been real nice to you, am I right?"

"You better leave now," Arthur said. "Your coffee is cold and we have just run fresh out."

"Sure, I understand," the oily blond man said. "She let you have a piece and you think you're Sir Galahad or somebody. But, brother, if you knew what I know . . ."

"Since you're a government agent, you'll be glad to talk to Robie Calkins. He is our sheriff here in Jackson County. Would you like to wait here for him? I'll give him a call right now."

"That's all right. I believe I've already found out what I needed to know. It's pretty clear she passed through here two years back." He laid a nickel on the counter and pushed it toward Arthur with one finger. "Here's what I owe."

Arthur pushed it back. "Keep it," he said. "I don't believe the coffee agreed with you."

The man smiled his twisted smile but did indeed rescue his nickel and make his surprisingly quick way to the door with an odd waddling stride. Arthur expected him to stop at the door and turn and make a last curdled remark, but he only pushed the screen open and stepped out into the late September sunlight that streamed saffron through the leaves of the big poplar there.

Arthur sighed tiredly and looked up and down the long room with its empty tables covered with red oilcloth and the big iron coal stove in the center of the aisle and the long counter with the five stools before it. When he emptied the remains of the coffee into the zinc sink behind him, he saw that his hands were shaking. He washed his hands and dried them on his apron and headed toward the storeroom in back to sit down and collect himself for a moment.

But Farley Redmon opened the kitchen door and called him back. "Arthur," he said, "could I talk to you just a minute?"

"Sure thing." He retraced his steps and when the older man held the door for him, he entered the kitchen.

"Sit down," Redmon said, indicating a tall wooden stool by the chop block. When Arthur sat, Redmon leaned back against the wall counter and folded his arms. "What was that all about with the little stout feller that come in?"

"I don't know," Arthur said. "He was asking questions about a woman I met one time."

"You got woman trouble, Arthur? Hard to believe."

"I've got an outstanding lack of woman trouble," he said. "It's hard for me to add up how much woman trouble I don't have."

"Ain't that kind of burdensome?"

"I just hope it's not fatal."

"Generally it ain't," Redmon said. "Not till some ornery husband stirs things up with a shotgun. You want to be careful now."

"I am careful," Arthur said. "I'm a careful man."

"Yes you are. That's the truth." Redmon produced a new package of Luckies from his shirt pocket, zipped it open, and tapped one out. He lit it with a kitchen match from a box on the counter. "I've been thinking about you," he said, "and how careful you are. I don't know what it was all about with that stout feller, but I thought you handled it okay."

"I don't usually drive away the customers."

"You did fine. You would've had your reasons." He looked into the cloud of smoke he exhaled toward the ceiling. "There's something I've been meaning to talk to you about. You know how it's been here at the café. Business is steady, what with the sawmill and the railroaders, but there ain't much profit. I've been trying to figure out how to do better by you, but I don't see no way I can come up with much more in terms of wages."

"That's all right," Arthur said. "I know how it is."

"Yeah. But you've been doing a good job. I don't know when I've seen a steadier man. I never could figure why you stuck."

"The arrangement suits me. I get time to write my stories."

"Your stories, yeah." Redmon tapped his ash into a soiled plate and smiled. "You know, I read one of your stories one time. I went down to the news store and bought one of them magazines and read it. Just to see. Beginning to end, I couldn't make head nor tail of it. It was about some animals on another world—that was all I understood. Do you believe there are other worlds with animals on them?"

"I don't know."

"The Bible don't say nothing about it. So it must be something you just make up in your mind, is that right?"

"The stories I write, I make up."

"You ever thought about writing a cowboy story, or something that people like more to read?"

"I'm not cut out for it," Arthur said. "I write the only kind of stories I'm able."

Redmon nodded. "Okay. The reason I ask, I always figured you were staying here till you made some big money with your writing and then you'd move on. If you did, I wouldn't know what to do. My boy Cletus ain't interested in this cafe and he ain't settled enough in mind to run it. I figure Cletus is just about ready to join the armed service, only he don't know it yet."

"Cletus is a good boy. He'll straighten out."

"I thought maybe if he got married, but then I got to studying on these women he's been running with. Ain't none of them would be any help. The trouble was losing his mother when he was little. I didn't have the furthest notion how to raise a youngun. So I reckon it's going to have to be Uncle Sam finishes the job."

"You're probably worrying about it too much."

"Well, I've worried myself gray-headed. Unless it's just natural age." He crushed his butt out in the littered plate. "Which was the other thing I was going to bring up. I don't want this business to go down the rathole. Someday Cletus might grow into it. Right now he don't want it, but later on he might. I want you to stay with me and help keep it going. Since I can't pay you better wage money, I thought I'd offer you an interest in the place. That don't mean much now, but when times lighten up it will. I can just about guarantee that."

"What do you have in mind?"

"Two percent to start with and then another percent every year till we get to ten. One of these days you'll find it was a good deal."

"But in order to get ten percent, I'd have to stay on another eight years."

"Yep."

"I'll have to think about it."

"That's all I want." Redmon offered Arthur his hand. "I just want your word you'll give it fair consideration."

"Sure I will. The offer means a lot to me." Arthur took Redmon's hard, dry hand and shook it twice gently. His own hand was soft and pulpy from washing dishes and he was beginning to grow flabby about the waist.

In fact, his health was none so sound as he had assumed. He learned from his army physical examination in 1942 that his teeth were in need of immediate repair and that one of the doctors thought he detected a heart murmur but

wasn't sure. At any rate, Arthur Strakl was turned down
for military service and rode in the bus back to Asheville
with a group of other rejects who were rowdy and gloomy
by turns. Then he took a westbound milk-stop bus to
Cherry Cove, trudged through the lonesome hamlet dark
at ten in the evening, went into his little hut, and fell asleep
without undressing, only dropping his scuffed brown shoes
by the bed.

When he woke next morning, he was still tired and all
his skin felt grimy. He took off his shirt and pants and
stumbled blindly to the tiny sink and ran water into a por-
celain basin and bathed as quickly and thoroughly as he
could. Then he placed a blue spatterware pot on his hot
plate and set about making coffee.

It was only when he sat at his writing desk sipping at
the strong unsugared coffee that he noticed how the big
armoire standing against the opposite wall had changed. It
was an ancient piece of work, this dim armoire, heavy oak
boards stained dark. Inside were Arthur's other three white
shirts and two pairs of pants and various socks and hand-
kerchiefs—the respectable wardrobe of a penurious orphan
bachelor. He always kept it neat and orderly, the way he
kept all his few possessions, the way he kept his life. His
life, like his little hut, was always prepared for visitation.

But now the visitation had occurred while he was absent. The doors of the armoire that had been stained almost
chocolate were now blue on the right side and violet on
the left. His Somewhere Doors had arrived. Arthur was so
profoundly gratified that tears trickled down his cheeks and
the back of his neck flushed red and warm.

They were not prepossessing. They were the same size
and shape as the armoire doors always had been; only the
color had changed. The surfaces were matte and cool to
the touch when he placed his hand flat against them. But
the texture of the surfaces was strange; the material didn't
feel like wood or metal or plastic. More like glass with a
subtle grain. He placed his ear directly against the blue door

and waited a long time but could hear nothing. Still the old chest seemed to breathe silently and steadily, like a great distant creature asleep.

He began to take stock. The room seemed otherwise unchanged, except that his clothing and other belongings had been taken from the armoire and carefully folded and laid out on his one other chair and on his bookcase. But there was a sheet of paper in the typewriter with a sentence cleanly typed in capital letters.

THANK YOU FOR YOUR VALUABLE EFFORTS

It was unsigned.

"My valuable efforts," Arthur said. He rubbed his eyes, brushing away the wetness. "I wish I could see what was so valuable."

He knew already that the presence of the Somewhere Doors would make an enormous difference, but he could not foresee what different shapes his life might take.

Now, though, he would have to choose. Before the doors arrived he had thought only vaguely about their contrasting possibilities; today the choice had become serious. Would he like to inhabit the golden utopian world that philosophers and visionaries over the centuries had guessed at? To immerse himself in the grandest productions of religious thought, scientific ingenuity, governmental peace, and aesthetic achievement of which human beings were capable? Or would he not rather live on the Garden Planet, the world brimful of pristine creation, the way our own must have been before Adam appeared? There as nowhere else he would be living in the very throb of the heart of existence, in the closest proximity to truth that his organism could endure.

He had been assured that neither world was noxious or dangerous, and he relied upon Francesca's word.

He knew, though, that the choice would haunt him, sleeping and waking, until it was actually made, and he knew, too, that he would have to watch himself closely so that the balance of his daily existence was not disturbed.

He would need to go on about his ordinary business as calmly and orderly as possible; only in this fashion could he make a wisely considered preference.

At this moment it came to him that there was a third choice. A third door, in effect: his own. He could choose to stay on the earth he knew and to go on with his life in Cherry Cove. Where before this obscure cranny of the universe had been a necessity, the haphazard lighting-down place of a kinless and disconnected man, now it assumed the dignity of election. He could choose to live here; he could choose to leave. He turned to look at the flimsy pine door of his little shack, warped and showing morning light at the jamb, and it seemed as strange to him and almost as inviting as the blue door and the violet.

When Cletus died at Anzio, the spirit of his father flickered violently and burned low. He was a man who rarely drank liquor, but during the months of February, March, and April of 1944, he was drunk almost every day. Arthur didn't mind that; he knew the frenzy would wear off. But he worried about what would happen when Redmon came to himself again. He couldn't think how the man might change.

After he stopped, it took another three weeks for him to dry out. He was sick the whole time, weak and shaking. Arthur ministered to him and gradually he began to eat normal meals and to drive his old Chevrolet pickup about and to tramp in the woods. One day he came into the café with a tinted photograph of Cletus under his arm, the one he'd gotten made with the boy in his uniform and overseas cap. When he climbed on a ladder to drive a nail and hang the picture on the wall behind the counter, Arthur knew that the old man had recovered and was going to make it.

For an old man was what he had become. His gray hair had whitened and his shirt hung loosely over his sunken chest; he had lost weight these last weeks. His eyes were watery behind his wire-rimmed bifocals and now and then

Arthur detected a nervous tic new to him: Redmon's head
would jerk suddenly to the left in response to some of the
remarks he heard people make. But Arthur was unable to
discern what kind of comment caused the reaction.

He took Arthur aside one evening in June when they
had finished cleaning up after the supper trade. He spoke
as plainly to his friend as he always did, telling him that
he regretted his lapse from duty during the last months. "I
hated to let go like that," he said. "But I knew it was either
drink or die. And I figured you would either stand by me
or you'd haul on down the line. My mind has got better
now. It ain't never going to be well again, but it has got
better. I probably wouldn't be here if you hadn't've helped
me out. So I'm having the papers drawn up for you to take
possession of one-third of the Red Man Café business. We
have started to make a little money here now and if we
can keep going for a while longer, there will be real money
in it. Not millions, you know that. But comfortable—you
can live comfortable."

"You must have known I'd stick with you in the hard
time. You knew that, didn't you?"

Redmon nodded. "I figured you would, but I didn't
know how bad it was going to be. To tell the truth, I still
don't know. I don't remember it real clear. But I expect I
was pretty far-gone."

"I was worried," Arthur said. "You came close to hurt-
ing yourself a couple of times."

"So I figured the best way to pay you back was to have
these papers drawn up. And there's something else in the
contract, too. It says that when I die, sole ownership of the
business will come to you."

"Wait a minute," Arthur said. "Don't you have some relatives somewhere to take exception to that?"

"I got a sister I don't know where in California. I don't
even know what her last name is these days. She'd have
five or six of them by now, I reckon. I got three cousins
and an aunt who will do fine on their own. You're about
the closest thing to real family I got left."

"I'm afraid I make a mighty scrawny family."

"Times is hard," Redmon said, and he actually smiled a small sad smile. "What do you say to my offer?"

"It's just like you for being generous, and a man would be a pure fool not to take you up on it. But this time again I'm going to ask you to let me think about it for a while."

"Sure. I'd expect you to."

"I'll tell you right now that I've got an opportunity that few people get. Nobody that I ever heard of, in fact. And it's more than likely that one of these first days I'll be gone from here. I don't know when. It depends on some decisions I need to make."

"You let me know about any offers you get. I'll do my best to match them."

"This is the kind of opportunity that can't be matched. And I won't be able to let you know beforehand. Once I'm ready to go, I'll just leave. You won't know where and you won't be able to find out. Don't worry, I'll be all right. I'll be exactly where I want to be. But you won't be able to get in touch."

Redmon's face darkened and his shoulders slumped. "Are you going to be leaving real soon? You could tell me that much, at least."

"I don't know. I would tell you if I could."

"Listen," Redmon said. "Why don't we dress up that ratty little shack you live in? Or why don't you just move out of it for good? If you get set up nice and comfortable, you might change your mind about leaving."

"No." He spoke as calmly and firmly as he knew how. "I'm doing all right where I am. I've got everything fixed just the way I want."

It had been seven years since he had laid eyes on the man he had named in his mind Ugly Dick, but as soon as he pushed into the empty café at three in the afternoon, Arthur recognized him. Time had left the dumpy little man almost untouched. His silver-blond hair had thinned so that his mottled scalp showed through and contempt had made the lines of his lips and eyebrows more deeply crooked. When he spoke, he showed teeth small and brown and yellow.

"Hello, sport," he said. "You remember me?"

"Yes," said Arthur, and reached behind him for a soiled rag and wiped the clean counter in front of the man. "Last time you were in here, our coffee didn't suit you. I don't know that it's changed much."

"I believe I'll try me a cup anyhow. It couldn't've got no worse."

"Price went up," Arthur said. "Prices are up everywhere."

"Even in Cherry Cola, North Carolina, huh?"

"Even in Cherry Cove."

He poured in cream and added three precise spoons of sugar and stirred. Then he lifted his head to peer at Arthur and give him that wildly crooked smirk. "I bet you remember our mutual friend, too, don't you?"

"You say you've got a friend?"

"Oh sure, you remember. Sheila Weddell. You wouldn't be forgetting her." He gave Arthur a soiled, heavy wink.

"I recall you asking about a woman. But I figured that you must do a lot of that, considering."

"Considering what?"

"Considering what a low-down son of a bitch you are."

The man's smile only grew more saturnine. "Still playing Sir Galahad, ain't you? But I got to tell you, sport, that there ain't no use in it anymore. You might be interested to see this newspaper story." He took a white envelope from his shirt pocket and laid it on the counter. When Arthur stood unmoving, content to give the man a long stare, he tapped it with a pudgy finger. "Go ahead and read it. I guarantee you'll find it interesting."

He picked it up. The headline read: WOMAN IN SPY SCANDAL COMMITS SUICIDE. The story was short and vague. A group of New York people were suspected of gathering in-

formation for "a foreign power." Arthur supposed that the
foreign power would be Russia, but the story was hazy in
all its details. Sheila Weddell, thirty-four, had been found
with her head in the gas oven of her apartment on Amster-
dam Avenue. There was no evidence of foul play. The police investigation was continuing.

The clipping did not reveal which newspaper had printed
the story. A photograph òf the woman was placed above
the headline and Arthur studied it intently. It was overex-
posed and the features were blurred. At first it looked a
little like the woman he knew as Francesca and then it
didn't. Then it did again.

"So what do you think of your sweetheart now, huh?"

"I never saw this woman in my life," Arthur said. He
took care in replacing the clipping in the envelope, then
laid it on the counter. "I hate to be such a big disappointment to you."

He produced a toothpick and put it between his front
teeth. "We know she passed some information on to you.
Something technical. We know you got brains. You don't
fool us, hiding away in this little possum-turd settlement.
We read them stories you write and I'll go ahead and tell
you, sport—we're right on the edge of busting your code.
We've just about got it figured out."

"My code?"

"Yeah. The hidden messages in that crazy horseshit you
write in them weird magazines. You don't think your buddies overseas are the only ones that can read, do you?"

"I don't know what you're talking about."

"Yeah. I was just real positive you wouldn't know what
I was talking about."

"I'm going to ask you again, just like last time, to show
me some identification," Arthur said. "If you're a government agent, I want to see what kind."

"What for? I ain't asking you for nothing. I'm telling you
about your girlfriend. That's all I came in for. I'll leave this
newspaper story with you, to maybe give you something

to think about." He stood up. "And a dime for the coffee, right?"

"Keep your damn dime. We don't want your money."

"Well now, that's mighty neighborly of you. So long, sport. Next time we meet it ain't going to be as pleasant as it has been."

"I'll bear that in mind," Arthur said. He watched the one enemy he ever knew he possessed waddle toward the door, his toothpick waggling up and down under his nose like a mechanical gadget. When he was gone, Arthur took fifteen cents from his pocket and rang the money into the cash register. He had just remembered that he still owed the café a nickel for the coffee Ugly Dick had ordered seven years before.

The next dawn found Arthur before his typewriter, struggling with a tale that was not progressing satisfactorily. He could not say why this particular story about visible creatures who inhabited an invisible planet was so difficult, but he had pottered with it two months now and it still didn't show signs of life. He sighed and stood up, arched his back and stretched his arms above his head. This mid-September morning, though still only pinkly lit by a pink sun, was full of life, cicadas and crickets sounding away and four roosters near and far voicing their victory over the nighttime.

He took up the envelope again for the dozenth time this morning and opened it and took out the clipping. Peering at it closely under the lamplight, he still couldn't tell. Was the woman in the photograph his Francesca? He would never be certain about the picture, he knew, and had decided simply to trust his instinct. He felt that the news story was about someone he didn't know.

The truth was, he didn't know anything. He didn't know who Francesca was or Ugly Dick, either. He would never understand what tangle of circumstance had bequeathed him the Somewhere Doors. He looked at them now, their colors still vivid, their surfaces still warmly and lightly pulsing with promise. One thing was certain: Ugly Dick with maybe some ugly help would have gotten into his hut and would have tried to open the doors and they had failed. Neither door would open even for Arthur until he made his fateful decision. Nor could they be damaged in any way.

He was forty-four years old now; he had grown middle-aged in this pleasure of indecision. They had hired a teenager to help wait tables and wash up at the café, so his work load had lightened, and his financial situation was secure, compared to the bone-scraping poverty he always had endured. His little hut was still brutally cold in winter and it was still an unhandy and often muddy trek to the outhouse at the edge of the field behind, but the Doors were here and their nearness supported him, comforted him, and never failed to entice with the dilemma they presented.

He slipped the clipping back into the envelope and laid it by his typewriter. Then he tugged on a light denim jacket and went out walking, stalking the dusty gravel road to the bridge and the river. The light was brightening now and a breeze came by as fresh as a cool hand across his forehead.

At the bridge he looked above the twisted waters into the swaying tops of the balsam trees and remembered meeting Francesca here in her white party frock and her white shoes. Maybe one of these days the smooth oxblood car would come darkly humming along again; maybe Francesca would step out. He turned to look, but the road was empty in both directions. Once more he sighed and began to retrace his steps to the hamlet.

On the bank by the bridgehead was a stand of six young silver-birch trees and beneath them a clump of knee-tall bright scarlet bee balm. He stopped for a moment to admire.

And then this scene—the lithe young trees with ragged bark fluttering, the brilliant red flowers nodding as the river purled—overwhelmed him. Almost every day he saw these things and did not see them, walking along absorbed. Anytime he liked he could remember this sight and yet he would always mostly forget. He burst into tears and went down in the road on the gritty gravel on his hands and knees, realizing that he had made his decision.

The sadness of utopia was the same sadness as that of paradise. Utopia and paradise could not remember. They were eternal and unaging and had no history to come to nor any to leave behind. They were dreams that Arthur for a long time had been experiencing with all his senses except those of his body. He had already opened both Doors and visited both Somewheres. He was ready to fling open wide the third door, the entrance to the world in which he already lived. Much had passed him by. Oh yes. Yet much awaited him still.

But right now and for five minutes longer he had no strength to rise. He remained on his hands and knees in the hard gray dirt of the road, weeping aloud like a child deceived or undeceived.

THE ADDER

 My Uncle Alvin reminds the startled stranger of a large, happy bunny. He is pleasantly rotund, and with silver-blond hair that makes him look a full decade younger than his sixty years. His skin has a scrubbed pink shine that the pale complexions of English curates sometimes acquire, and he has a way of wrinkling his nose that one irresistibly associates with—well, I've already named rabbits. He is a kindly, humorous, and often mildly mischievous fellow.

My admiration of Uncle Alvin has had a large measure of influence upon my life. His easygoing manner has seemed to me a sensible way to get along in the world. And his occupation is interesting and leisurely, though it's unlikely he'll ever gain great wealth by it. I can support this latter supposition by my own experience: I followed my uncle into the antiquarian book trade and I am not—please let me assure you—a rich man.

We don't compete with one another, however. Uncle Alvin lives in Columbia, South Carolina, and runs his mail-order business from his home. The bulk of my trade is also mail order, but I run it from a shopfront in Durham, North Carolina. My shop sells used paperbacks, mostly to Duke University students; in the back I package and mail out rare and curious books of history, the occult, and fantasy, along with some occasional odd science fiction. Uncle Alvin specializes in Civil War history, which in South Carolina almost guarantees a living income, however modest.

But anyone in the trade is likely to happen upon any sort of book, whether it belongs to his specialty or not. When Uncle Alvin called one Saturday morning to say that he had come into possession of a volume that he wanted me to see, I surmised that it was more in my line than his, and that he thought I might be interested in making a purchase.

"What sort of book is it?" I asked.

"Very rare indeed—if it's genuine. And still rather valuable if it's only a forgery."

"What's the title?"

"Oh, I can't tell you that on the telephone," he said.

"You can't tell me the title? It must be something extraordinary."

"Caution never hurts. Anyway, you can see it for yourself. I'll be by your place with it on Monday morning. If that's all right with you."

"Say, that's grand," I said. "You'll stay overnight, of course. Helen will be thrilled to see you."

"No," he said. "I'm driving through to Washington. I'll stop off on the way. Because I don't want to keep this book in the car any longer than I have to."

"We'll have lunch, at least," I said. "Do you still crave lasagne?"

"Day and night," he replied.

"Then it's settled," I said, and we chatted a little longer before ringing off.

*   *   *

Monday morning he entered my shop—called Alternate Histories—carrying a battered metal cash box and I knew the book was inside it. We sounded the usual pleasantries that friendly kinfolk make with one another, though ours may have been more genuinely felt than many. But he was anxious to get to the business he had in mind. He set the cash box on top of a stack of used magazines on the counter and said, "Well, this is it."

"All right," I said. "I'm ready. Open her up."

"First, let me tell you a little bit about what I think we have here," he said. "Because when you see it, you're going to be disappointed. Its appearance is not prepossessing."

"All right."

"In the first place, it's in Arabic. It's handwritten in a little diary in ordinary badly faded ink and it's incomplete. Since I don't read Arabic, I don't know what's missing. I only know that it's too short to be the full version. This copy came to me from the widow of a classics professor at the University of South Carolina, an Egyptologist who disappeared on a field excursion some thirty years ago. His wife kept his library all this time, hoping for his return. Then, last year, she offered up the whole lot. That's how I happen to be in possession of this copy of *Al Azif.*"

"I never heard of it," I said, trying not to show the minor disappointment I felt.

"It's the work of a medieval poet thought to have been insane," Uncle Alvin said, "but there is debate as to how crazy he actually was. His name was Abdul Alhazred and he lived in Yemen. Shortly after composing *Al Azif* he met a violent and grisly death—which is all we know about it because even the eyewitnesses dispute the manner of his dying."

"Abdul Alhazred. Isn't that—?"

"Yes indeed," he said. "The work is more recognizable under the title of its Greek translation, *The Necronomicon.*

And the most widely known text—if any of them can really be said to be widely known—is the thirteenth-century Latin translation of Olaus Wormius. It has always been surmised that the original Arabic text perished long ago, since every powerful government and respected religious organization has tried to destroy the work in all its forms. And they have largely succeeded in doing so."

"But how do you know what it is, if you don't read Arabic?"

"I have a friend," he said proudly. "Dr. Abu-Saba. I asked him to look at it and to give me a general idea of the contents. When I handed it to him and he translated the title, I stopped him short. Better not to go on with *that*. You know the reputation of *The Necronomicon*."

"I do indeed," I said, "and I don't care to know what's in it in any detail. In fact, I'm not really overjoyed at finding myself in such close company."

"Oh, we should be safe enough. As long as we keep our mouths closed so that certain unsavory groups of cultists don't hear that we've got it."

"If you're offering it to me for sale—" I began.

"No, no," he said hastily. "I'm trying to arrange to deposit it in the Library of Congress. That's why I'm going to Washington. I wouldn't put my favorite nephew in jeopardy—or not for long, anyway. All I would like is for you to keep it for a week while I'm negotiating. I'm asking as a personal favor."

I considered. "I'll be happy to keep it for you," I said. "To tell the truth, I'm more concerned about the security of the book than about my own safety. I can take care of myself. But the book is a dangerous article, and an extremely valuable one."

"Like an atomic weapon," Uncle Alvin said. "Too dangerous to keep and too dangerous to dispose of. But the Library of Congress will know what to do. This can't be the first time they've encountered this problem."

"You think they already have a *Necronomicon*?"

"I'd bet money," he said cheerfully, "except that I wouldn't know how to collect. You don't expect them to list it in the catalogue, do you?"

"They'd deny possession, of course."

"But there's a good chance they won't have an Arabic version. Only one is known to have reached America and it was thought to have been destroyed in San Francisco around the turn of the century. This volume is probably a copy of that version."

"So what do I do with it?" I asked.

"Put it in a safe place. In your lockbox at the bank."

"I don't have one of those," I said. "I have a little old dinky safe in my office in back, but if anyone came to find it, that's the first place they'd look."

"Do you have a cellar in this shop?"

"Not that I'd trust the book to. Why don't we take a hint from Edgar Allan Poe?"

He frowned a moment, then brightened. "A purloined letter, you mean?"

"Sure. I've got all sorts of books scattered about in cardboard boxes. I haven't sorted them yet to shelve. It would take weeks for someone to hunt it out even if he knew it was here."

"It might work," Uncle Alvin said, wrinkling his nose and rubbing his pink ear with a brisk forefinger. "But there's a problem."

"What's that?"

"You may wish to disregard it because of its legendary nature. I wouldn't. In the case of *Al Azif,* it's best to take every precaution."

"All right," I said. "What's the legend?"

"Among certain bookmen, *The Necronomicon* is sometimes known as *The Adder.* Because first it poisons, then it devours."

I gave him a look that I intended to mean: not another one of your little jokes, Uncle Alvin. "You don't really expect me to believe that we've got a book here that eats people."

"Oh no." He shook his head. "It only eats its own kind."

"I don't understand."

"Just make sure," he said, "that when you place it in a box with other books, none of them is important."

"I get it," I said. "Damaged cheap editions. To draw attention away from its true value."

He gave me a long, mild stare, then nodded placidly. "Something like that," he replied at last.

"Okay," I agreed, "I'll do exactly that. Now let's have a look at this ominous rarity. I've heard about *The Necronomicon* ever since I became interested in books. I'm all aflutter."

"I'm afraid you're going to be disappointed," Uncle Alvin said. "Some copies of this forbidden text are quite remarkable, but this one—" He twitched his nose again and rubbed it with the palm of his hand.

"Now don't be a naughty tease, Uncle Alvin," I said.

He unlocked the metal box and took out a small parcel wrapped in brown paper. He peeled away the paper to reveal a rather thin octavo diary with a worn morocco cover that had faded from what would have been a striking red to a pale brick color, almost pinkish. Noticing the expression on my face, he said, "See? I told you it would be a disappointment."

"No, not at all," I said, but my tone was so obviously subdued that he handed it to me to examine without my asking.

There was little to see. The pinkish worn binding felt smooth. The spine was hubbed and stamped *Diary* in gold, but the gold, too, had almost worn away. I opened it at random and looked at incomprehensible Arabic script so badly faded that it was impossible to say what color the ink had been. Black or purple or maybe even dark green—but now all the colors had become a pale uniform gray. I leafed through almost to the end but found nothing in the least remarkable.

"Well, I do hope this is the genuine article," I said. "Are you sure your friend, Dr. Hoodoo—"

"Abu-Saba," said Uncle Alvin primly. "Dr. Fuad Abu-Saba. His knowledge of his native tongue is impeccable, his integrity unassailable."

"Okay, if you say so," I said. "But what we have here doesn't look like much."

"I'm not trying to sell it. Its nondescript appearance is in our favor. The more undistinguished it looks, the safer we are."

"That makes sense," I admitted, handing it back to him.

He glanced at me shrewdly as he returned it to the cash-box, obviously thinking that I was merely humoring him—as to a certain extent I was. "Robert," he said sternly, "you're my favorite nephew, one of my most favorite persons. I want you to follow my instructions seriously. I want you to take the strongest precautions and keep on your guard. This is a dangerous passage for both of us."

I sobered. "All right, Uncle Alvin. You know best."

He wrapped the volume in the brown paper and restored it to the scarred box and carried it with him as we repaired to Tony's Ristorante Venezia to indulge copiously in lasagne and a full-bodied Chianti. After lunch he dropped me back at Alternate Histories and, taking *Al Azif* out of the metal box, gave it over to my safekeeping with a single word of admonition. "Remember," he said.

"Don't worry," I said. "I remember."

In the shop I examined the book in a more leisurely and comprehensive fashion. But it hadn't changed; it was only one more dusty, faded, stained diary like thousands of others and its sole distinction to the unlearned eye was that it was in handwritten Arabic script. A mysterious gang of sinister thieves would have to know a great deal about it merely in order to know for what to search.

I decided not to trust it to a jumble of books in a maze of cardboard boxes. I took it into my little back-room office, shoved some valueless books out of the way, and laid it flat on a lower shelf of a ramshackle bookcase there that was cluttered with every sort of pamphlet, odd periodical, and assorted volume from broken sets of Maupassant, Balzac, and William McFee. I turned it so that the gilt edge faced outward and the word *Diary* was hidden. Then I deliberated for a minute or two about what to stack on top of it.

I thought of Uncle Alvin's warning that no important books were to be placed with *Al Azif* and I determined to heed it. What's the point in having a favorite uncle, wise and experienced in his trade, if you don't listen to him? And besides that, the dark reputation of the book was an urgent warning in itself.

I picked up an ordinary and utterly undistinguished copy of Milton's poems—Herndon House, New York, 1924. No introduction and a few sketchy notes by an anonymous editor, notes no doubt reduced from a solid scholarly edition. It was a warped copy and showed significant water damage. I opened to the beginning of *Paradise Lost* and read the first twenty-six lines, then searched to find my favorite Miltonic sonnet, number XIX, *On His Blindness*.

> *When I consider how my light is spent*
> *Ere half my days, in this dark world and wide,*
> *And that one Talent which is death to hide,*
> *Lodg'd with me useless, though my Soul more bent*
> *To serve therewith my Maker, and present*
> *My true account, lest he returning chide . . .*

Well, you know how it goes.

It's a poem of which I never tire, one of those poems that has faithfully befriended me in periods happy and unhappy since the years of my majority. Milton's customary stately music is there, and a heartfelt personal outcry not often to be found in his work. Then there comes the sternly contented resolution of the final lines. Milton requires, of course, no recommendation from me, and his sonnet no encomium. I only desire to make it clear that this poet is important to me and the sonnet on his blindness particularly dear.

But not every copy, or every edition, of Milton is important. I have personal copies of fully annotated and beautifully illustrated editions. The one I held in my hand was only a cheap mass edition, designed in all probability to be sold at railway bookstalls. I placed it on top of the Arabic treasure and then piled over both books a stack of papers from my desk, which is always overflowing with such papers: catalogues, book lists, sale announcements, and invoices. Of this latter item especially there is an eternal surplus.

Then I forgot about it.

No, I didn't.

I didn't in the least forget that I almost certainly had in my possession *Al Azif,* one of the rarest documents in bibliographic annals, one of the enduring titles of history and legend—and one of the deadliest. We don't need to rehearse the discomfiting and unsanitary demises alleged of so many former owners of the book. They all came to bad ends, and messy ones. Uncle Alvin had the right idea, getting the volume into the hands of those prepared to care for it. My mission was merely a holding action—to keep it safe for a week. That being so, I resolved not to go near it, not even to look at it until my uncle returned the following Saturday.

And I was able to keep to my resolution until Tuesday, the day after I'd made it.

The manuscript in its diary format had changed when I looked. I noticed right away that the morocco covers had lost their pinkish cast and taken on a bright red. The stamped word *Diary* shone more brightly, too, and when I opened the volume and leafed through it, I saw that the pages had whitened, losing most of the signs of age, and that the inked script stood forth more boldly. It was now

possible to discern, in fact, that the writing actually was
clothed in different colors of ink: black, emerald green,
royal purple, Persian rose.

The Necronomicon, in whatever version, is a remarkable
book. All the world knows something of its reputation, and
I might have been more surprised if my encounter with it
had been uneventful than if something unusual transpired.
Its history is too long, and a knowledgeable scholar does
not respond to mysterious happenings in the presence of
the book by smiting his breast and exclaiming, "Can such
things be?"

But a change in the physical makeup of the book itself
was something I had not expected and for which I could
not account. Not knowing yet what to think, I replaced it
just as it had been, beneath the random papers and the
copy of Milton, and went on with my ordinary tasks.

There was, however, no denying the fact of the changes.
My senses did not belie me. Each time I examined it on
Tuesday and Wednesday—I must have picked it up a
dozen times all told—our *Al Azif* had grown stronger.

Stronger: As silly as that word seems in this context, it is
still accurate. The script was becoming more vivid, the
pages gleamed like fresh snowbanks, the staunch morocco
covers glowed bloodred.

It took me too long to understand that this manuscript
had found something to feed upon. It had discovered a
form of nourishment that caused it to thrive and grow
stout. And I am embarrassed to admit that more hours
elapsed before I guessed the source of the volume's
food—which had to be the copy of Milton's poems I had
placed on top of it.

Quickly then I snatched up the Milton and began to examine it for changes. At first I could discover no anomalies.
The print seemed perhaps a little grayer, but it had already
been rather faded. Perhaps, too, the pages were more brittle
and musty than I'd thought—but, after all, it was a cheap
book some sixty-odd years old. When I turned to the open-

ing of *Paradise Lost,* all seemed well enough; the great organ tones were as resonant as ever:

> *Of Man's First Disobedience, and the Fruit*
> *Of that Forbidden Tree, whose mortal taste*
> *Brought Death into the World, and all our woe . . .*

And I thought, Well, I needn't have worried. This poetry is immune to the ravages of time and of all circumstance. So it was in anticipation of a fleeting pleasure that I turned idly to glance at sonnet XIX:

> *When I consider how my loot is spent*
> *On Happy Daze, a fifth of darling wine . . .*

But the familiar opening of the sonnet had lost much of its savor; I was missing something of that intimate stateliness to which I was accustomed. I set down my pallid reaction to tiredness and excited nerves. Anxiety about Uncle Alvin's treasure was beginning to tell on me, I thought.

I shook my head as if to clear it, closed my eyes and rubbed them with both hands, then looked once more into the volume of Milton open on the counter, sonnet XIX:

> *When I consider how my lute is bent*
> *On harpy fates in this dork woolly-wold,*
> *And that dung-yellow witches' breath doth glide,*
> *Lobster and toothless . . .*

No use—I was too confused to make sense of the lines at all. It's only nerves, I thought again, and thought, too, how glad I would be for my uncle's return on Sunday.

I laid the copy of *Al Azif* down and determined to put the puzzle out of my mind.

I couldn't do that, of course. The idea had occurred that our particular copy of Abdul Alhazred's forbidden work was changing the nature of Milton's lines. What was it Uncle Alvin had compared it to? An adder, was it? First it poisons, he'd said, then it devours. Was it indeed poisoning the lines of the great seventeenth-century poet? I took up the Milton again and opened to the beginning of his immortal religious epic:

> *Of Man's First Dish of Beetles, and the Fat*
> *Of that Forboding Fay, whom Myrtle Trent*
> *Brought fresh into the World, and Hollywood* . . .

The words made no sense to me, none at all—but I couldn't remember them any differently than how they appeared on the page. I couldn't tell whether the fault lay in the book or in myself.

A sudden thought inspired me to go to my poetry shelves and find another edition of Milton's poems so that I could cross-check the strange-seeming verses. If *Al Azif* truly was changing the words in the other, then a book untouched by the diary would render up only the purest Milton. I went round to the front and took down three copies of Milton's poems in different editions and used my favorite sonnet as touchstone. The first one I examined was Sir Hubert Portingale's Oxbridge edition of 1957. It gave me these lines:

> *When I consider to whom my Spode is lent,*
> *Ear-halves and jays on this dark girlie slide* . . .

It seemed incorrect somehow. I looked at the poem in

Professor Y. Y. Miranda's Big Apple State University Press
volume of 1974:
"Winnie's Corn Cider, how my lust is burnt!"
That line was wrong, I felt it in my bones. I turned to
the more informal edition edited by the contemporary poet
Richmond Burford:

> *When I consider how a lighter splint*
> *Veered off my dice in this dour curled end-word*
> *And that wan Talent . . .*

I shook my head. Was that correct? Was it anywhere
near correct?

The trouble was that I couldn't remember how the lines
were supposed to read. I had the vague feeling that none
of these versions was the right one. Obviously, they
couldn't all be right. But why couldn't I remember my favorite poem, more familiar to me than my Social Security
number?

Uncle Alvin's warning had been "First it poisons, then it
devours."

Now I began to interpret his words in a different way.
Perhaps *The Necronomicon* didn't poison only the book it
was in physical contact with, perhaps it poisoned the actual
content of the work itself, so that in whatever edition it
appeared, in whatever book, magazine, published lecture,
scholarly essay, commonplace book, personal diary—in
whatever written form—a polluted text showed up.

It was an altogether terrifying thought. Uncle Alvin had
not warned against placing it with an important *edition;* his
warning concerned an important *book.* I had placed it with
Milton and had infected the great poems wherever they
now might appear.

Could that be right? It seemed a little farfetched. Well
no, it seemed as silly as picturing Milton, the poet himself,
in a Shriner's hat. It seemed just dog-dumb.

But I determined to test my wild hypothesis, nevertheless. I got to the telephone and called my old friend and
faithful customer in Knoxville, Tennessee, the poet Ned
Clark. When he said hello, I was almost rude: "Please don't
ask me a lot of questions, Ned. This is urgent. Do you have
a copy of Milton's poems handy?"

He paused. Then: "Robert, is that you?"

"Yes it is. But I'm in an awful hurry. Do you have the
poems?"

"In my study."

"Can you get the book, please?"

"Hold on," he said. "I have an extension. I'll pick up in
there." I waited as patiently as I was able until he said,
"Here we are. What's the big deal?"

"Sonnet XIX," I said. "Would you please read it to me?"

"Right now? Over the phone?"

"Yes. Unless you can shout very loud."

"Hey, man," he said. "Chill out, why don't you?"

"I'm sorry, Ned," I said, "but I think I may have made
a big mistake. I mean, a heavy *bad* mistake, old son. So
I'm trying to check up on something. Could you read the
poems to me?"

"Sure, that's cool," he replied, and I heard him leafing
through his book. "Okay, Robert. Are you ready? Here
goes: 'When icons in a house mild lights suspend, Or half
my ties in this stark world have died . . .'"

I interrupted. "Okay, Ned. Thanks. That's all I need to
hear right now."

"That's all? You called long distance to hear me say two
lines of your favorite poem?"

"Yes I did. How did they sound to you?"

"As good as Milton gets."

"Did they sound correct? Are those the words as you've
known them all your life?"

"I haven't known them all my life," he said. "You're the
wild-haired Milton fan. He's too monumental for my taste,
you know? I mean, massive."

"Okay, but you've read the poem, at least."

"Yes indeedy. It's a big-time famous poem. I read all those babies, you know that."

"And these lines are the ones you've always known?"

Another pause. "Well, maybe not exactly," he admitted. "I think the punctuation might be a little different in this book from what I'm used to. But it mainly sounds right. Do you want publication information?"

"Not now," I said, "but I may call back later for it." I thanked my friend and hung up.

It seemed that my surmise was correct. All the texts were now envenomed. But I wanted to make certain of the fact and spent the next four hours telephoning friends and acquaintances scattered throughout America, comparing the lines. Not every one answered, of course, and some of my friends in the western states were groggy with sleep, but I got a large enough sample of first lines to satisfy me.

Walt Pavlich in California: "One-Eye can so draw my late sow's pen . . ."

Paul Ruffin in Texas: "Wind I consider now my life has bent . . ."

Robert Shapard in Hawaii: "Wound a clean liver and the lights go out . . ."

Vanessa Haley in Virginia: "Wind a gone slider and collide a bunt . . ."

Valerie Collander in West Virginia: "Watch a corned beef sandwich bow and bend . . ."

These were enough and more for me to understand the enormity of my mistake. All the texts of Milton that existed were now disfigured beyond recognition. And I had noted a further consequence of my error. Even the texts as they resided in memory were changed; not one of my friends could remember how the lines of sonnet XIX were *supposed* to read. Nor could I, and I must have been for a decade and a half one of the more constant companions of the poem.

The copy of *Al Azif* was flourishing. I didn't need even

to pick it up to see that. The gilt edge shone like a gold bar
fresh from Fort Knox and the morocco binding had turned
ruby red and pulsed with light like a live coal. I was curious how the inks would glitter, so now I did pick up the
volume—which seemed as alive in my hands as a small
animal—and opened it at random.

I was right. The different colors of the inks were as vivid
and muscular as kudzu and looked as if they were bitten
into the thick creamy pages like etching. However disquiet-
ing these changes, they had resulted in a truly beautiful
manuscript, a masterpiece of its kind. And though I knew
it to be a modern handwritten copy, it also seemed to be
regaining some of its medieval characteristics. Most of the
pages were no longer totally in Arabic; they had become
macaronic. Toward the end pages a few English words
were sprinkled into the Eastern script.

Oh, no.

As long as *Al Azif* was in Arabic it was relatively harmless. Most people would be unable to read the spells and
incantations and the knowledge to be found there that
is—well, the traditional epithet is *unspeakable,* and it is ac-
curately descriptive. I certainly would not speak of the contents, even if I was able to read them.

I flipped to the front. The first lines I found in the first
page were these:

Wisely did Ibn Mushacab say, that happy is the tomb
where no wizard hath lain, and happy the town at night
whose wizards are all ashes. For the spirit of the devil-in-
dentured hastes not from his charnel clay, but feeds and
instructs the very worm that gnaws. Then an awful life
from corruption springs and feeds again the appointed scav-
engers upon the earth. Great holes are dug hidden where
are the open pores of the earth, and things have learned to
walk that ought to crawl.

I snapped the cover shut. Those phrases had the true
stink of *The Necronomicon*. You don't have to be an expert
upon the verses of Alhazred to recognize his style and subject matter.

I had read all of these pages that I ever wanted to read,
but even so I opened the volume again, to the middle, to
confirm my hypothesis. I was right: *Al Azif* was translating
itself into English, little by little. There was only a sprinkling of English in the latter pages; the early pages were
English from head to foot; the middle pages half Arabic,
half English. I could read phrases and sentences, but not
whole passages. I could make out clearly, "they dwell in
the inmost adyta"; then would follow lovely Arabic callig-
raphy. Some of the passages I comprehended were these:

*Yog-Sothoth knows the gate; in the Gulf the worlds them-
selves are made of sounds; the dim horrors of Earth; Iä ïa
ïa, Shub-Niggurath!*

Nothing surprising, and nothing I wanted to deal with.
But I did understand what had happened. When I had
so carelessly allowed this copy of *Al Azif* to batten upon
Milton's poetry, it took the opportunity to employ Milton's
language in the task of translating itself. With a single
thoughtless act, I had given *The Necronomicon*—call it accursed or unspeakable or maddening, call it whatever mi-
natory adjective you choose—both life and speech and I
saw the potential for harm that I had set in place.

I flung the volume into my flimsy little safe, clanged shut
the door, and spun the dial. I put up the CLOSED sign on
my shop door, called my wife, Helen, to tell her I wouldn't
be home, and stood guard like a military sentinel. I would
not leave my post, I decided, until Uncle Alvin returned to
rescue me and all the rest of the world from a slender little
book written centuries ago by a poet who ought to have
known better.

Nor did my determination falter.

As soon as Uncle Alvin laid eyes on me Sunday morning, he knew what had gone wrong. "It has escaped, hasn't it?" he said, looking into my face. "*Al Azif* has learned English."

"Come in," I said. When he entered, I glanced up and down the empty street, then shut the door firmly, and guided my uncle by his arm into my office.

He looked at the desk, at the crumpled brown paper bags that held my meals and at the dozens of empty Styrofoam cups. He nodded. "You set up a watch post. That's a good idea. Where is the volume now?"

"In the safe," I said.

"What's in there with it?"

"Nothing. I took everything out."

"There's no cash in the safe?"

"Only that book you brought upon me."

"That's good," he said. "Do you know what would happen if this copy was brought into contact with cash money?"

"It would probably poison the whole economy of the nation," I said.

"That's right. All U.S. currency everywhere would turn counterfeit."

"I thought of that," I said. "You have to give me some credit. In fact, this never would have happened if you had given me a clearer warning."

"You're right, Robert, I'm sure. But I feared you'd think I was only pulling your leg. And then I thought maybe you'd experiment with it just to see what would happen."

"Not me," I said. "I'm a responsible citizen. *The Necronomicon* is too powerful to joke around with."

"Let's have a look," he said.

I opened the safe and took the volume out. Its outward appearance was unchanged, so far as I could tell. The ruby morocco was rich as a leopard pelt and the gilt edge and gold stamping gleamed like fairy-tale treasure.

When I handed it to Uncle Alvin, he didn't bother to glance at the exterior of the book, but turned immediately to the latter pages. He raised his eyebrows in surprise, then began reading aloud: "'The affair that shambleth about in the night, the evil that defieth the Elder Sign, the Herd that stand watch at the secret portal each tomb is known to have and that thrive on that which groweth out of the tenants thereof: All these Blacknesses are lesser than He Who guardeth the Gateway—'"

"Stop, Uncle Alvin," I cried. "You know better than to read that stuff aloud." It seemed to me that it had grown darker in my little office and that a certain chill had come into the room.

He closed the book and looked at it with a puzzled expression. "My word," he said, "that is an exotic and obsolescent diction. What has *Al Azif* been feeding on?"

"Milton," I answered.

"Ah, Milton," he said, and nodded again. "I should have recognized that vocabulary."

"It has poisoned all of Milton's works," I said.

"Indeed? Let's see."

I picked up one of the copies on the desk and handed it to him.

He opened it and, without showing any expression, asked, "How do you know this book is Milton?"

"I brought all my copies in here and stacked them on the desk. I've been afraid to look at them for two days, but I know that you're holding a fairly expensive edition of John Milton's poetic works."

He turned the open book toward me. The pages were blank. "Too late."

"It's eaten all the words," I said. My heart sank. I tried to remember a line of Milton, even a phrase or a characteristic word. Nothing came to mind.

"Well, maybe not *eaten*," Uncle Alvin said. "Used up, let's say. *Absorbed* might be an accurate term."

"No more Milton in the world. . . . How am I going to

live my life, knowing I'm responsible for the disappearance of Milton's works?"

"Maybe you won't have to," he replied. "Not if we get busy and bring them back."

"How can we do that? *Al Azif* has—swallowed them," I said.

"So we must get the accursed thing to restore the poems, to spit them up for us, the way the whale spat Jonah whole and sound."

"I don't understand."

"We must cause this manuscript to retract its powers," he said. "If we can reduce it to its former state of weakness, the way it was when I first met it in Columbia, the works of John Milton will reappear on the pages—and in the minds of men."

"How do you know?"

"You don't think this is happening for the first time, do you? It has been such a recurring event that restoration procedures have been designed and are followed in a traditional—almost ritualistic—manner."

"You mean other authors have been lost to it and then recovered?"

"Certainly."

"Who?"

"Well, for instance, the works of all the Cthulhu Mythos writers have been lost to the powers of the evil gods that they describe. Stories and poems and novels by Derleth, Long, Price, and Smith have all had to be recovered. The works of Lovecraft have been taken into the domain of *Al Azif* at least a dozen times. That's why his work is so powerfully pervaded by that eldritch and sinister atmosphere. It has taken on some of the shadow of its subject."

"I never thought of that, but it makes sense. So what are the restoration procedures?"

"They're simple enough," he said. "You keep watch here while I go to my car."

He gave me the book and I set it on the edge of the desk,

well away from any other written matter. I couldn't help thinking that if Uncle Alvin succeeded in defeating the powers of *Al Azif* and rescuing the hostage works of Milton, these moments represented my last opportunity to read in the great bibliographic rarity. And simply as a physical object it was inviting: The lush red glow of the binding offered a tactile pleasure almost like a woman's skin and I knew already how the inks shone on the white velvety pages. *The Necronomicon* seemed to breathe a small breath where it lay on the desk, as if it were peacefully dozing like a cat.

I couldn't resist. I picked it up and opened it to a middle page. The seductive Persian rose ink seemed to wreathe a perfume around the couplet that began the fragment of text: "That is not dead which can eternal lie, And with strange aeons even death may die." A large green fly had settled on the bright initial that stood at the beginning of the next sentence, rubbing its legs together and feasting on the ink that shone as fresh and bright as dripping blood. I brushed at it absentmindedly and it circled lazily toward the ceiling.

"That is not dead . . ."

The lines sang hypnotically in my ear, in my head, and I began to think how I secretly longed to possess this volume for myself, how indeed I had burned to possess it for a long time, and how my ridiculous rabbit-faced Uncle Alvin was the only obstacle in my way to—

"No, no, Robert," Uncle Alvin said from the doorway. "Close the book and put it down. We're here to break the power of the book, not to give in to its spells."

I snapped it shut in a flash and flung it onto the desk. "Wow," I said. "Wow."

"It's an infernal piece of work, isn't it?" he said complacently. "But we'll have a hammerlock on it shortly."

He set down the metal cash box he had formerly carried the book in and opened it up. He then laid *The Necronomicon* inside and produced from a brown paper bag under his arm a small book bound in black cloth and placed this second book on top of the other and closed the metal box and locked it with a key on his ring. I noticed that the black book sported no title on cover or spine.

"What are we doing now?" I asked.

"The inescapable nature of this book is to cannibalize other writings," he said. "To feed upon them in order to sustain its ghoulish purposes. If it is in contact with another work, then it *must* try to feed; it cannot stop itself. The method of defeating it is to place it with a book so adamantine in nature, so resistant to evil change, to the inimical powers of darkness, that *The Necronomicon* wastes all its forces upon this object and in exhausting itself renders up again those works it had consumed earlier. It simply wears itself out and that which formerly had disappeared now reappears."

"Are you certain?" I asked. "That seems a little too simple."

"It is not simple at all," he said. "But it is effective. If you'll open up one of your copies of Milton there, we ought to be able to watch the printed words return to the pages."

"All right," I said, and opened one of the blank-paged books to a place toward the front.

"The process is utterly silent," he said, "but that is deceptive. Inside this box, a terrific struggle is taking place."

"What is the unconquerable book that you put in with it?"

"I have never read it," he said, "because I am not worthy. Not yet. It is a great holy book written by a saint. Yet the man who wrote it did not know he was a saint and did not think of himself as writing a book. It is filled with celestial wisdom and supernal light, but to read it requires many years of spiritual discipline and ritual cleansing. To read such a holy book one must first become holy himself."

"What is the title?"

"Someday soon, when I have accomplished more of the

necessary stages of discipline, I will be allowed to say the title aloud," he told me. "Till then I must not."

"I am glad to know there is such a book in the world," I said.

"Yes," he said. "And you should look now to see if Milton is being restored to us."

"Yes he is," I said happily. "Words are beginning to reappear. Wait a second while I find our control poem." I leafed through rapidly to find sonnet XIX and read aloud:

> *"When I consider how my light is spent*
> *Ere half my days—"*

"Why are you stopping?" he asked.

"It's that damned pesky green fly again." I brushed at the page. "Shoo!" I said.

The fly shooed, lifting from the book in a languorous circle, buzzing around the office for a moment, and then departing the premises through the open window there beside a broken bookshelf.

"You need to put in a screen," Uncle Alvin said. He wrinkled his nose, pawed at his ear.

"I need to do a lot of things to this old shop," I replied. "Let's see now, where were we?" I found my place on the page and began again:

> *"When I consider how my light is spent*
> *Ere half my days, in this dark world and weird—"*

"Wait a minute," my uncle said. "What was that last word?"

I looked. *"Weird,"* I said.

He shook his head. "That's not right."

"No, it's not," I said. "At first I didn't see it was wrong because the fly covered it, the same old fly that was gobbling up the ink in *The Necronomicon.*"

"A carrier," he said slowly. "It's carrying the poison that it contracted from the ink."

We looked at each other and, as the knowledge came clear to me, I cried out: *"The fly!"* Then, just as if we had rehearsed to perform the single action together, we rushed to the window.

But out there in the sleepy southern Sunday morning would be countless indistinguishable green flies, feeding, excreting, and mating.

EMBER

When I came out of Paradise, they were shooting at me. Shotguns and pistols mostly, whatever they could grab hold of. I jumped into my old green pickup truck in the parking lot and drove off. I couldn't shoot back because I'd already pitched my .44 pistol away. I wouldn't have shot back anyway, so I stepped on the gas. Probably it was rocks thrown up against the undercarriage, but it might have been bullets hitting the truck, so I ducked my head down.

Scared, hell yes, I was scared. Couldn't breathe except in gulps and my hands were shaking and two drops of dead-cold sweat inched from my armpit down my left side. It wasn't so much getting shot at—though I hear tell you never get used to that—but the faces of the people, faces of them that used to be my friends and neighbors turned red and murderous. I couldn't stand up to that.

Ten minutes later I felt a little easier and stopped trembling so much, not seeing the headlights after me in my mirror. But I knew they'd be coming and I knew they'd already called the sheriff and the highway patrol. I was a wanted man now, the only time in my life. I didn't know what to think.

I had already made one big mistake. If I had turned right coming out of the parking lot there at West End Tavern Dance, I'd be traveling toward the broad highways, the ones that connected with Georgia and all the other states and all the nations of the world. But I'd turned left instead and there was nothing in front of me but the brushy mountains of western North Carolina, briar thickets and tear-britches rocks over the steep slopes. And especially there was Ember Mountain, where nobody went in the dark, nobody that would anyhow talk about it in the daylight.

But I started thinking maybe some things wouldn't be so bad. I had fished the streams around here and knew my way some, and the more the men that were trailing me didn't know Ember, the better. So I made a turnoff onto a little clay road that goes up Burning Creek and crosses it three times. At the third ford the trail's no wider than a cow path, and I pulled the truck over into a stand of laurel and cut the motor and the lights and opened the door.

Then it was like stepping into another world because the silence came down so sudden and the darkness. The world of Paradise township where I'd shot with my .44 my untrue sweetheart Phoebe Redd was sure enough a world away, I was thinking, and then the silence let up a little and I could hear the hood of the truck ticking as the motor cooled and the feathery swishing of the wind in the treetops and the low mutter of Burning Creek off to my left. Those noises brought me back to myself and how I had to keep running.

I scrambled down to the edge of the creek and got down on all fours and drank like a dog, tasting the mountain in the water, the mossy rocks above me in the dark and the humus and the secret springs of Ember. When I stood up again, I could hear the other night sounds of late August, the crickets and cicadas and somewhere a long way off to my right the long-drawn empty call of a hoot owl.

But there was nowhere to go but up the mountain. The farther I got in the nighttime, the farther away I'd be come sunup. Let them try to find me in six hours, or eight. Carolina wouldn't hold me, nor Georgia, either, once I got past Ember Mountain.

I dreaded to have to do it, though. It wasn't only what they say about the ridges and hollers of Ember, and I'd heard plenty of that and put stock in some of it. But just any old mountain in the dark of the night is a reckless time, and if there hadn't been so many certain dangers behind me, I wouldn't have been traveling on to meet new ones.

So I started up, my pants wet and my feet soaked in my shoes. My breath began to pound in my chest and my knees felt weak, but I climbed any way I could, tripping over tree roots and crawling on all fours and sliding down on the loose shale; it was a wonder I didn't just tumble to the bottom and lie at the end of the valley like a rag doll a little girl has lost on her picnic.

But I kept on going and the rocks and roots and bushes kept tearing at me. The left side of my face got laid open by a bramble or a twig and I could feel the blood oozing down my neck into my shirt. I had to stop and rest a lot of times, but I didn't like to and it got worse the higher I climbed because the silence got deeper and I began to remember more and more what folks said about Ember.

Oh Phoebe, I thought, oh Phoebe Redd. See what your faithless ways have brought on me.

I went on. I kept going till I thought I couldn't stand it anymore and then I came to the backbone of a stony ridge and struck south along it, still climbing and climbing till I came to a weedy clearing. Then I saw a point of orange light up the mountain to my left. The more I tried to make it out, the more I couldn't see it clear. That's the way it is in the dark silence with trees everywhere.

But when I climbed some more, not breathing as hard

now, I saw it again, clean and shining but shadowed over by something every now and again so that it flickered. I figured it to be a hunter's camp fire, even though I had not heard his dogs running. Not everybody was scared of the tales and there was a plenty of game varmints up here; I could tell that just by listening.

I started toward the light. Not a wise decision, maybe, but it wasn't like I decided. A picture in my mind drew me: I could see how there'd be a fellow there by his camp fire and how he'd have coffee or a sip of whiskey and maybe both. I was hot and cold and sick of the rocks and the bruising. I'd make up some lie to tell him about what I was doing up here, any lie that would stick.

But the ridge led down before it led up, and going downhill in the dark without a trail is a fool's job. Rocks and sawbriars all the way down and then a slick mud gulley at the bottom, then laurel thicket when I was climbing again, as puzzledy as a roll of barbwire. But I could just smell that coffee and taste it in my mouth, so I kept on and on. Might be a hunting man would appreciate some company up here in the lonesome midnight. Or it might be he wouldn't. It was a chancy notion.

But then when I came to the edge of the clearing, I found it was no camp fire. Here was a neat mountain cabin with a hearth fire inside and the clearing about me was for a garden. I could make out the shape of the cabin pretty well. It was a clean place, the shingle roof mossed over, the little porch propped up on flat rocks. From the chinked rock chimney rose the ghost-colored smoke of the fire I'd spied so far away.

I waited at the edge, watching and listening. There were no dogs. I took it strange there were no dogs. A man at midnight walking up to a house in the solitary woods—he expects to hear the hounds begin to racket and come out to meet him.

Who was it lived here, anyhow? Nobody I'd ever heard about.

I tried to walk quiet, but they'd have to be stone-deaf in there not to hear me rustling and crackling through the goldenrod and the cornstalks. But I came right to the side of the house without anybody raising a holler and saw that it was just a cabin like many another I know. Weathered oak boards and mud-chink rock foundations and on the porch flowers growing in lard buckets and a cane-bottom rocking chair empty but for starlight and shadow. There was silence all around.

On this side there was a little square window curtained with dotted swiss, just above eye level. I stretched up on tiptoe to see inside.

The room was neat and cheery in the firelight. There was a hooked rug on the floor and another bigger one hanging on the wall and two little tables with dried flowers in vases and a couple of straight chairs. There was a tall, dark rocking chair beside the fire and in it sat a little old granny woman with iron-colored hair. She was wearing a washed-pale blue gingham dress and a blue-gray apron. She wasn't rocking in her chair, just sitting there as still as a tombstone, but she was not asleep. I could see the firelight glinting yellow in her eyes like they were cat's eyes.

I let down flat on my feet to ease my legs. It was nothing strange to see, an old woman remembering in front of her fire, but I had to wonder. How could it be only her up here and no menfolk about to help her do? It all looked all right, but when I thought, there was nothing right about it.

I decided to take another look and this time it wasn't an old woman in her rocking chair but another kind of thing hard to tell about. All gnarled and rooty like the bottom of a rotted oak stump turned up. Or all wattly, the way the toadstools will grow on fallen timber. Maybe more like it looks at the bottom of a candle burnt halfway down, where the wax has gathered in smooth pulpy lumps.

I can't say exactly because it was nothing exact to see. Something alive that nobody would ever think could live, something that knew about me out here by the window

without seeing me, something that was an old woman in
a chair and was no old woman any way in the world.

All right, Bill Puckett, I thought. This is what comes of
your jealous murdering. You have landed in the hardest
place a man can land.

I figured that maybe my third glimpse might be the true
one and when I peeped again, it was the same old woman
as before, sitting just the way she was at first, with her eyes
still shining yellow and not rocking in her rocking chair.

So maybe I'd imagined the rooty thing there, tired and
scared as I was, and I was determined to get the good of
her hearth fire, no matter. Ember Mountain with its ditches
and brambles was too much for me this night; I was willing
to take my chances with the old woman.

I went around to the front and up the five worn porch
steps, trying to fix on a lie to tell her and whoever was
with her here. I rapped three times and thought I heard a
"Come in," but the door planks were mighty thick. Anyhow, I shot back the smooth-handled latch and entered.

When she craned her head to look, it came to my mind
what a sorry marvel I must appear. I was all wet and
muddy and my clothes were ripped and one side of my
face and neck was probably still bleeding from a gash. Not
a handsome sight to look on.

But she didn't show the least surprise. "Come in," she
said. "Come to the fire where it's warm."

I was grateful. I crossed over to the clean rock hearth
and held my hands palm-up to the fire, the way you can't
help doing. I warmed one side of myself and turned to
warm the other.

She was looking me up and down. "You appear to been
a good while in the woods," she said.

"Yes ma'am, I have been."

"Even on a summer night you can get cold and tore up
on this mountain."

"Yes ma'am."

She was just a nice old granny woman. Even with her sitting down, I could tell she was real short. Short and thick, I thought, before I observed she was a humpback woman. I couldn't place her age, the skin of her face being so smooth and ruddy. Apple cheeks, folks call that, but she was old. Her hands were wrinkled and looked powdery and her voice was shrewd and trembly with her years.

"You got to be careful," she said. "There's many a good man been lost on Ember in the night."

"Yes ma'am."

She turned her head sideways and the firelight caught in her eyes till they shone like pieces of gold. "Why are you up here, then, so late into the night?"

I hadn't made up my lie yet and now when I tried to, I couldn't do it. It stuck in the middle of my throat and I coughed and choked. I couldn't make sense in my head except just the truth and finally that was what I told her. "The law is after me," I said, "and some other people, too. They're wanting to hang me on a big hickory tree, I reckon."

"What for?"

"I shot a woman," I said.

"Did you kill her?"

"*I* don't know. But it was an awful big pistol I pulled the trigger on."

"Who was she?"

"She was just a woman that treated me wrong. There ain't no use to say her name."

"Sit down," she said. "Pull up a chair to the fire and sit you down. It's good you told me the straight of it and not some infernal lie."

I felt better leaning forward in the chair and soaking up the heat. My pants legs were steaming as the denim dried. "I didn't take no pleasure in it," I said. "It just came over me too powerful. When I went to the West End Tavern Dance, I saw them both and I shot and threw down my pistol and fled away."

"Wasn't it Phoebe Redd, this woman?"

"How did you know that? How could you ever hear about it up on this mountain?"

Her voice dropped to a mumble and it was hard to hear her. I thought she said, "Because it's not the first time, never ever the first time."

"What did you say?" I asked.

She looked at me then with a look as straight as a broomstick. "How old a man would you be?"

"My name is Bill Puckett," I told her. "I'm twenty-seven years old."

"Ain't you surely old enough to know better about women?"

"It came over me. I was in a fever where I couldn't think."

She nodded and got up and limped to the fire, showing she had a bad leg. She took up a big wrought-iron poker and shifted the three logs. Red and orange sparks went up fantail and the wood snapped and sizzled. Her bunched-up shadow divided into three on the walls. "Well, what's done is done," she said. "What you'll be doing next, that's the question."

"I don't know anything to do but to just keep running," I said. "Because all they're going to do is just keep coming after me."

"You could give up and hand yourself over."

"I don't know," I said. "They're riled pretty hot. No telling what they might do to me."

"Sit you back," she said, "and take your ease. I've got some herb tea already made that I can warm up for you. It'll take some of the ache out of your bones."

I didn't say her no but began to rub my ankles and the calves of my legs. My skin was itching where my pants legs dried by the hearth fire.

With her heavy poker she swung the iron crane out from the fireplace wall over the blaze and lifted down a black kettle from the adze-scarred mantelpiece beam. She hung

the kettle on the crane hook. "Take off your shoes and
your stockings," she said, and when I did, she drew them
to the hearth with the poker and arranged them to dry.
"Won't take a minute for the tea to warm," she said. "A
good strong herb tea. Here now, move over into my rocking chair and rest a little easier."

I did that, too, and began to unloosen a little in my muscles. I leaned back and looked into the fire and then when
I looked at her again, she blurred in front of me because
of the firelight. I put it down to the firelight. "You'll need
you a cup and saucer," she said. "I'll go and get them from
the kitchen."

I tried to get up.

"You just stay here. You'll be needing all the rest you
can get."

I listened to her shuffling about and I wondered again
about her being lame and how she managed up here on
the mountainside all alone by herself. I wondered, too, a
great deal about how she heard of Phoebe, only I expected
she had a radio back there in the kitchen that she would
listen to a-nights, though I hadn't seen any power lines
when I found the house. But the fact that she knew the
name of Phoebe Redd just showed how soon they'd be
catching up with me.

I must have dozed a little because next I remember her
face close to mine, her apple cheeks smooth and reddish,
and her eyes away from the firelight not yellow now but
black-dark as two soot spots. And something I hadn't seen
before: There were dents in her skin here and there, two
in her forehead and one in her left cheek just below the
eye and three dents in her throat, little pushed-in places
like the thumbprints you'd leave in biscuit dough. The skin
was smooth in the dents, smooth as isinglass. Wounds that
have healed over, I thought, old wounds. Except for one
in her throat just under her chin: That one was healed but
looked fresh, too, as red and rare as a scarlet flower.

She's had a bad time, too, I thought, and right then that
was all I thought.

"Here now," she said. "Drink this all down." She offered
me a china saucer with little blue painted flowers and a gilt
edge and on it a blue enamel cup almost brimful of steaming tea. I remember the look of that cup and saucer as clear
as the bluest sky. "It'll be good and strong for you," she
said.

I knew I'd spill it if I tried to hold the saucer, my hands
unsteady as they were. I set the saucer on the floor and
held the cup in my thumb and first finger by its fragile little
handle. When I sipped at it, the taste of its heat went right
to my breastbone. It was strong and rank and bitter and it
tasted of something that reminded me of *far away*. That is
the best I know how to tell: It tasted of *far away*, every bit
as strong as she had said. Just the steam lifting out of the
cup clambered in my head.

"There now," she said. "Can you feel anything from
that?"

"It's mighty good," I said.

She was standing close over me again, her face almost
touching mine and looking deep into my eyes. "Go on.
Drink it down."

I didn't want to look into her eyes, so it was her throat
I saw, the red new-healed smooth place beneath her chin.
Right then I recognized that wound for the first time as the
place on her body where my .44 bullet had struck my de-
ceitful Phoebe back in Paradise. It was the exact same spot.

I wanted to understand that; I wanted to try to make
some sense, but it was too late. The old woman's tea was
too strong in me and the little china cup slipped out of my
unnerved fingers onto the hearthstones. It didn't break into
a hundred splinters; it stuck solid and quivering on the
rock like an arrow shot into a tree trunk. I stared at it there
unharmed.

I kept staring at the cup because I didn't want to look at
the granny woman. It shivered my body to know if I
looked at her I'd see her again all ugly roots and lumps
and with her firelit yellow eyes deformed.

But that's what I knew and not what I saw. All I saw was a heavy black roaring before my eyes and a sick shaking and I dropped then into a deep swoon, the deepest I reckon that a man can endure.

And when I came back to myself, I was not sitting in the rocking chair and there was no hearth before me and not even a cabin around me. I was lying flat on my back under the stars in the middle of a fair-sized grassy bald, a circle with edges so sharp against the trees and bushes, it looked like it was cut here with a knife.

It took a long time for me to get steady and sit up and when at last I do, I find you-all here, all twelve of you men sitting cross-legged on the edge of the circle, all watching me with your wild eyes.

And when one of you, the tall, dark-complected man there in his ancient buckskins, asked me to tell my whole story, I didn't hold back the least little crumb of it. Awful as it is, it's the truth and I know you know that.

Because you don't need to explain anything to me. I can see in your bitter faces and in the bitter shadows of your eyes how it is and how it is going to be, that we are the men who ever killed Phoebe Redd; over the years and generations and centuries it was us that left the marks of our pistol balls on her again and again. Mine was the freshest one just beneath her chin, as red as a scarlet rose. I know how her revenge on us is everlasting and how we are to be scattered howling to and fro on the mountain; and how there is no rest for us and no surcease, but only being driven miserable on the rocks and thorns until Ember Mountain perishes and time itself passes all away.

DUET

 I know what I'm supposed to be telling you. I'm supposed to say that I wish for peace everywhere in the world and, true enough, I do. But it's not the kind of thing I've got any special right to say.

I'd rather tell you about Caney Barham, if you didn't mind. I know you never heard of him. He was only just a friend of mine that shot himself, but if I was to try to answer your question with the truth, I would be talking about Caney.

Not on purpose. He was never a man to shoot himself on purpose. It was surely an accident, though they had to guess what took place from the way things were left lying. He was found held upright, tangled in a barbwire fence, with his .22 rifle lying on the ground close by and an empty shell casing in the chamber. His wife, Frances, found him about seven-thirty on a Thursday evening. What evidence there was pointed to this idea of what took place: That sometime between six and seven right during twilight,

Caney had heard his chickens making a racket and got to thinking some varmint had got in to molest them; and then he'd gone into the bedroom and reached the .22 off the wall and loaded and cocked it and then walked around back to the fence that enclosed the chicken pen; and then, figuring to sneak up on the skunk or king snake or whatever it was, he'd tried to clamber through the fence instead of opening the squeaky gate; and then while he was putting his leg through the strands, the rifle went off and killed him instantly. It had to be instantly because the wire hadn't cut him up the way it would if he had been struggling in agony. The bullet went in under his chin and lodged low in the back of his head.

That's what they told me the county coroner said, and I didn't want to know even that much. I never looked on Caney dead; I never asked a question about the way it must have happened. But you never need to ask; there's always somebody glad to talk about those things.

The first I heard about it was that same night around nine. I'd got home from the sawmill and taken a bite of supper and was putting new strings in my guitar when John Newsome called me on the telephone and told me Caney had shot himself in the head and it looked to be an accident.

I said, "Oh Lord. How is he, John?"

And he said, "He's dead, Kermit. I understand he's passed away."

Then in a little while I said "Oh Lord" again, and "Thank you, John, for calling to tell me." Then I hung up the telephone and went back to messing with the guitar, not getting anything done, my fingers only fussing with it. The idea hadn't really got into my mind yet, you see, and then in a minute or two when it did, I pushed the guitar away from me and sat there on the edge of the bed and moaned out loud. "Oh oh oh."

We were buddies since I could remember. We went to grade school together and to high school and when we finished with that we went to the sawmill to drive trucks for old man McCracken. We spent a lot of hours together, even though Caney got married and Frances gave him an awful smart little girl, and I never have married. We fished together and hunted and many a night he'd come to my house or I'd go to his, and we'd sit till the morning hours shone bright, sipping a little moon, me playing the guitar and Caney singing along with me, and laughing at ourselves till we were near sick of it. We never drank heavy, being moderation men, but we'd sip and carry on and the time eased away.

And now he was dead.

I knew he was dead, but it didn't feel to me like he was gone, and to this day it never has and maybe it never will. Really passed away, I mean, so that I knew I'd never see him again. Maybe because he was so brimful and overflowing with high spirits, a lean brown man with deep brown eyes. When he grinned, easy always, his teeth shone white and his brown eyes lit up like a cat's will glow in the low light. There was nobody didn't like him except a few there's no pleasing ever, the kind that will not like anybody. He was full of devilment, and all of it harmless as far as I could see, practical jokes that wouldn't hurt a housefly and some silly sayings he was attached to. Like when we were driving the two-ton along and would come to a railroad crossing. "There's been one through here," he would say. "I've found his tracks." Or if he saw a fine-looking young girl walking by, he'd say, "There goes Good Morning Judge and Hello Jailhouse." I can see how these might not be the world's funniest jokes, but when Caney said them, the way he would every time without fail, he'd lean back in the truck seat and laugh like he'd thought them up on the spot.

He wasn't anything wild, just anxious for a good time, and he wouldn't mind a little hardship if he thought a good time might come with it.

Like the time he made the dare. It was one Thursday in

early June he said, "Now you and me are going camping
this weekend, and all we're going to take with us is our
sleeping bags and our shotguns and two shells apiece and
six kitchen matches. If we're going to eat anything, that's
all we'll have to get it with. And now we'll see what kind
of stuff we're made of, old son."

That's what we did.

It didn't turn out all that well, to tell the truth, and I
don't know but what I might have been ashamed to tell
anybody if it wasn't for Caney. Because he told everybody
and laughed at the tale on us as much as if it was on anybody else. We went up to Blue Meadows, off to the right
of Clawhammer Gap, and we tramped those weedy wet
fields from five-thirty in the morning till four-thirty in the
afternoon and we saw no game, not a particle, unless you
count in butterflies and grasshoppers. I got so hungry I
wanted to suck the moss off the rocks. Then about four-
thirty a big old ugly crow came flapping overhead and Caney brought up his shotgun and down it came. He looked
at me and I looked at him. Then we both looked at the
crow. Then he grinned that grin. "Kermit, old buddy," he
said, "it's like I foretold. Going to see what kind of stuff
we're made of."

We worked down to the last match before we could get
a fire going, and we plucked that crow without benefit of
water and roasted it on sticks. The meat was as tough and
black as a patent-leather shoe, and I won't try to tell how
it tasted, except that a steady diet of it is bound to slow
down your worst glutton. Like I say, I wouldn't have told,
but when we came back down to the valley, Caney could
find no peace till everybody he met heard about us eating
crow. I mean, eating *crow*.

So now I sat there on the edge of the bed and moaned.
The sorrow had reached down into me. I didn't cry any
tears, but I could feel in my chest and stretching up to the
back of my throat a hard something like a bar of iron, so

that I couldn't swallow or breathe properly. I sat for a long time, rocking back and forth with my hands twisted in my lap. When you hear somebody close has died, you act on that sentence, even if you know the blackest sorrow is going to come later.

Memories flashed into my head and I didn't try to keep them away, because I knew I couldn't. Caney bent over his reel, cussing a backlash . . . Caney showing off a brand-new hunting jacket he'd saved up for forever . . . Not drawn-out put-together thoughts, but little bright pictures. Like when he dipped his finger in a bucket of honey we'd brought from a bee tree and held it out for his little girl, Aline, to lick, stretched up on her tiptoes.

After a while I started to sort out what I was supposed to be doing. What I wanted to do was nothing but go off to the woods and tramp till some of the pain went away. But that wouldn't be right. There would be people who would want to talk to me and I ought to find out if there was anything I could do for Frances. I didn't relish the prospect of talking to a bunch of people I wouldn't much know. A tragedy fills up a house with strangers. Still and all, there was no way out for me.

I put on a clean shirt and stepped into my old Dodge pickup—The Nutbucket, Caney used to name it—and drove to the head of Big Sandy Cove, where the neat little Barham house was. Already the driveway and the shoulders of the narrow gravel road were filled with trucks and cars. I had to park a good hundred yards away and walk up, counting six cars I didn't recognize.

Lights were on in every room but one. In the light from the living room windows I saw Preacher Garvin standing in the front yard under the big red maple. He was wearing a white shirt and tie and he'd had to come a pretty far piece, so I supposed he'd heard about Caney a while before I did. When I came trudging by, he stopped me.

"Is that you, Kermit Wilson?"

"It's me, Preacher."

"Come here, son, a minute."

I went and he laid his hand on my shoulder and struck up talking in a hushy voice. He had chewing gum in his mouth, and there's nothing strange about that, but it hit me odd right then, the way piddling things will do in such a time, and I kept staring at the way his mouth worked and not much attending what he said. Then I pieced it out that he was telling me the story of what had happened, all the way from the rifle on the bedroom wall to the arrival of the sheriff, who had to come out to any gunshot wound, and then the one doctor in our county who was also the coroner. Then he told me about having to send a car over to Caney Creek to tell his mother because she didn't have a telephone, and I hadn't recollected till now that Caney had been named after the place he was born and how he used to say jokes about that, too.

Then Preacher Garvin took his hand off and stood back and gave me that straight-on look that ministers have got down pat. "You boys were pretty close, weren't you?"

"Yes sir," I said. "We were close."

"An awful shame," he said. "Young man like Caney, all his life ahead of him."

"Yes sir."

"In the midst of life we are in death."

And what can you say to that? I know it's the way preachers have to talk, but I never know how to act when they do. So I just shook his hand and walked on up into the house.

The living room was crowded but quiet. It was mostly women in there, the elder women who always come when somebody is taken, sitting without moving except now and again to pull their shawls tighter around their shoulders, though the room was boiling already. The three men present looked mighty uncomfortable and I nodded to them. I didn't see Frances; one of the ladies told me she was lying down in the back bedroom, that the doctor had given her a sedative. The little girl, Aline, had been sent to her Aunt

Margaret's house down on Little Sandy and would be staying there till the funeral on Saturday. I started to ask how
come they knew so soon the time of the funeral, but didn't.
They'd been through this so many times, they knew everything needful to know.

Aunt Purdie Swann asked me if I wanted anything to
eat, but I reckoned not. "You could drink some fresh coffee
then, couldn't you?"

But I wasn't going to let her make me take anything.
"No ma'am," I said. "It wouldn't set well."

I stepped out the door onto the porch and stood there
in the shadow, breathing deep. The living room had nigh
overpowered me with the worn-down hooked rug and the
family pictures on the end tables and the blue and yellow
picture of Jesus on the wall and the old record player in
the corner that would sometimes go and sometimes
wouldn't. Too many nights Caney and I had talked and
sung in that room, and the hard feeling in my chest grew
harder, and I had to get out.

I stood in a patch of darkness and lit a Camel and pulled
at it and realized that this was the first cigarette in a long
time that wasn't a habit only but a comfort. I tried to think
what worldly good I was doing here, with Frances and
Aline not around, nor anybody else that Caney and I'd had
much truck with. I decided I make an awful poor social
mourner and flipped my butt into the yard and went down
the steps, ready to head home.

Preacher Garvin stopped me again. "Not leaving us, are
you, Kermit?"

"I guess so. I don't see what I can do here."

"Yes. These things are mostly in the hands of the wom-
enfolk. How are they bearing up in the house?"

"All right, I reckon. The doc has got Frances lying down
to rest."

"That's good. I guess you know we'll be having the services on Saturday afternoon in the church."

"All right."

He stepped closer and lowered his voice. "I was thinking something over, Kermit. You and Caney used to like to get together and make music, didn't you?"

"Yes sir, we did." Those words made me flinch, *used to*.

"I was thinking it might be fitting for you to give the opening hymns for the service. I know it could be a hardship, but would you be willing to sing?"

I took a deep breath. This was the first thing that had come up that I could do for Caney, but I didn't know if I could get through a song with him lying by me in his coffin. "Preacher Garvin," I said, "I can give you maybe one hymn. Never in this world could I sing two."

"One is all right," he said. "One is just fine. What would you care to sing? Didn't Caney have some hymn he held special? One that would be proper for a funeral service?"

"We liked a whole lot of hymn tunes," I said. "I don't know which would be the right one for his laying-away."

"All right. You think on it and call me tomorrow."

"Yes sir."

I went along and got into my pickup and drove away. It occurred to me I might drive the thirty miles over to Plemmonsville to the Ace High Grill, where Caney and I used to go now and then to drink six bottles of beer and hear Mac Wiseman or Don Reno on the jukebox. But that would just make me feel more lonely. Everything I thought of made me feel bad.

I drove home. I went into the bedroom and took up the guitar and this time I strung it. I tuned it, twisting the keys, testing the strings over and over. I got it in perfect tune before I went to sleep.

Friday I laid out of work. I didn't want to see the people we worked with every day, I didn't want to hear what they'd be saying, and I did not want to answer questions. Seeing I wasn't part of Caney's family, old man McCracken might well dock my pay. Well, let him. He'd done it before and I didn't starve. Maybe I never wanted to work again.

I put on my red wool shirt and my hunting boots and warmed up a cup of coffee and drank it while cleaning my .12-gauge. Then I got into my tan jacket and found my cap and went out. I didn't carry any shells; the heart wasn't in me to be killing. I just wanted the gun solid in my hands as I walked along.

It was the early April season with the air crisp and cool and the sky scrubbed blue. The first minute I set foot in Colter's Grove I felt better. I liked the pine needles springy underfoot and the smell of trees and the sunlight coming through in rags and the silence everywhere about, the silence I could feel on my skin at first. I walked a long time, not following a true path, just keeping my feet where they would make the least noise. After half an hour it looked like I was heading toward Ember Mountain, and I figured I could climb if I desired, setting one foot before the other and feeling no strain, not today.

When I came to Burning Creek at the foot, I decided not to climb. I knelt and cupped up three mouthfuls of water in my hand and then sat on a rock on the creek bank with my shotgun across my knees. There I sat for the longest time. The comfort to me here was the sound of the water rolling over the stones. That's a clean sound to listen to for hours, always the same but never exactly the same one minute to the next. A sound going on forever but with little changes inside it that never exactly repeat. You can make it louder or softer while you listen just by the way you concentrate. If a musical group, especially one with a good banjo or mandolin, could capture some of this creek sound and get it right, they would be famous and folks would come from anywhere to hear them. There are musicians who can make sounds of every kind, the wind in the treetops and freight trains picking up speed and fox hunts on the mountain top, but I never heard anyone try to get the creek sound down.

I sat and listened. Little by little the hard iron went out of my sadness. All night I'd had bad dreams I couldn't re-

member except they left my mind dark, and now that darkness lightened. I wasn't reconciled and I surely was not
happy, but I didn't have that cold, bitter taste in my throat.
I'd come out to the place of purest sadness, sad but free
and floating, sad but natural-feeling. It was fitting and
proper how I felt now, and I knew for the first time I'd be
able to sing and it wouldn't unman me with Caney lying
by.

I sat a while longer and then got up and walked home.
The sun was higher now and the day was getting warm.

In the house I stowed my shotgun and hung up my
jacket and cap and unlaced my boots partway. Then I went
into the front room and dialed Preacher Garvin. His wife
answered and then went off to fetch him.

"Hello?"

"Hello, Preacher. This is Kermit Wilson."

"Yes, all right. How are you doing, son?"

"Okay, I reckon. A little better than I was."

"That's right," he said. "Good. The Lord disposes. He gi-
veth and He taketh away."

"Yes sir."

"What can I do for you, Kermit?"

"Well, I believe I've decided I can sing at the funeral all
right."

"That's fine, that's mighty fine. Have you decided what
number?"

"Yes sir. That is, I've got one I know will be all right,
but about the other one I don't think you'll be pleased."

"What is it?"

"One hymn he liked awful well was 'Peace in the Valley.' And it's a good song for baritone and I believe I can
handle it."

"Fine," he said. "Be hard to think of one more suited to
this time of trial."

"The other one I kind of doubt," I said. "It was his favorite song and that's the reason I want to sing it. He never
got enough of it. We might sing it five times in a night now
and then."

"Which one are you talking about?"

"'Roll in My Sweet Baby's Arms,'" I said.

"No."

"I know it's not a hymn tune."

"And you know well enough already you can't sing that. You're talking about a secular song."

"It was the song he liked the best."

"I wouldn't mind stretching it some if you wanted to do a good old-time church shout, something like that. But the one you're talking about you can't sing in church."

"It's the one he'd want to hear."

"There's other people to think about. Caney's kinfolks and Frances and her kin and the church members."

"Caney Barham," I said. "He's the one I'm studying on right now."

He didn't answer right away, then said, "Well, I don't see how. There might be one way to work it out, but seeing as how you're one of the pallbearers . . ."

"Not me. I'm not going to be a one to put him in the ground."

"I didn't know that. I just naturally had you down on the list."

"I think John Newsome would take my place."

"Well now, if John would do that, you might sing your song afterward. Not as part of a Christian funeral service, no sir, but if you wanted to sing it at the grave site after the service is over and the last prayer is prayed, I wouldn't be able to stop you. It looks like you're bound and determined."

"Yes sir."

"Then that's the way it'll be. I'll pass the word in private so if anybody wants to stay on they can. But I can't announce it in a church and I can't stay myself."

"Ever how you like, Preacher," I said. "I am not anxious for people to stay on."

"All right then," he said. "Now at the service you'll be singing first, after Juney McClain stops playing the piano

for people to come in by. And that's all the arrangements
we need to make. See you tomorrow at two o'clock."

"Yes sir," I said, and we hung up.

I arrived early at the church and parked around back. I
didn't want to have to shake hands. I wanted to keep to
myself until I started singing. There was a momentful thing
inside me, something important not to harm, and I had to
keep it like that or I would never be able to bring off what
I was setting out to do in the necessary way.

So I went through the side door into the little anteroom
beside the choir stall and unpacked my guitar and tested
the tuning. Then did nothing but sit and wait. I had dressed
in fresh tan cotton pants and a white shirt and my dark
brown suit jacket and a blue necktie, and this was the closest thing to a full dress outfit I had. If I'd had one, I would
have put on an Opry singer's outfit, with piping and copper
buttons and a big cowboy hat; that's the kind of rig Caney
would appreciate. But back then I'd never even seen one
of these outfits in person.

I heard Juney McClain start playing the piano, soft and
slow and out of rhythm like always, and I could hear the
scuffle and whisper of the people sliding into the pews.
Then Preacher Garvin came in and stopped and adjusted
his black string tie and said, "You doing all right, Kermit?"

"Yes sir."

"That's fine. You just follow me out. I'll go to the po-
dium and when Juney stops playing, I'll give you a nod.
After you're finished, you turn around and go sit in the
choir stall and I'll start the service."

"All right."

I followed him out, gazing at his heels till I got where I
was supposed to stand. When I looked up at the congrega-
tion, I was fearful I'd never get it done. I caught a glimpse
of Frances and Aline and Caney's mother on my left-hand
side and heard the mumbles and sobs and whimpers and I
cut my eyes away and wouldn't look that way again. I

knew almost everybody else out there but I didn't look into their faces.

There was one fellow I didn't know, somebody I'd never laid eyes on before. He was dressed in a dark expensive-looking suit and seated in one of the back pews. He leaned forward with his hands draped over the empty pew in front of him and on one wrist was a shiny watch and the sun gleamed on it, making a silver patch, burning white. I decided that while I was singing I would rest my eyes on this gleam.

I looked at Preacher Garvin and he nodded and I began.

Now "Peace in the Valley" is not a tricky song to sing and, like I'd said, a good song for the baritone voice. But being easy is what makes it hard, because you're likely to want to throw your voice around and fancy it up. I'd made up my mind to treat it right, to make it clear and strong and simple. I wanted to hit the notes as telling as a clock striking.

And when I started, that full momentful thing I'd been feeling since yesterday at the foot of Ember Mountain took hold of me. My whole body was at ease and my voice came out in a way I'd never heard before. It was like it wasn't my voice but another person standing at my right-hand side and singing away unconcerned while I accompanied him on the guitar. I didn't understand what was happening, but I thought, Probably this is the last time. Maybe I'll never sing again after today.

When I had finished, I turned and walked to the choir stall, unstrapping as I went. I laid the guitar down as easy as I could on the varnished oak seat, because the church had gone as quiet as the midnight sky. Even the sobbing and whimpering had hushed.

A long time it seemed to me passed before Preacher Garvin said, "Thank you, Brother Kermit, for that fine rendition, just mighty fine."

Those were his last words I heard, and not even one from the funeral service. I sat there pondering the days gone by forever and how I'd come to sing the way I did, and then once more Caney Barham alive and the things we used to say and do. I believed that if he heard me sing "Peace in the Valley," he liked the way I did it and was soothed.

The time came at last when the service was over and the casket was to be carried out to the little graveyard beside the church. The bearers shouldered it and the family followed them, moaning now again and crying, and then the rest of the people. I waited in the anteroom, tuning the strings again and watching through the window till I saw the procession had got through the gate. Then I went out and followed, keeping well behind.

From the grave, too, I kept my distance. They set the casket down and Preacher Garvin read prayers I couldn't hear and then they lowered Caney into the deep red ground and sprinkled dirt on him by the handful. Finally the preacher led away the family and five or six others. They didn't look at me standing over to the side as they went by. They were pretending I was not there.

But a lot of people stayed, and when I walked up to the grave and the mound of loamy clay, they stepped back and spread out a little. I was surprised because I hadn't expected anybody to linger on. Even the stranger with the shiny wristwatch was there; he had a square black leather case hanging by a strap from his shoulder and I took it to be some kind of radio or camera. I thought maybe I ought to say something, to explain that I meant no sin and no shame, that I was singing only my buddy a memorial.

It was a warm day, the sky as blue as ever you'll see, and a warm light breeze over the slopes. I didn't look at anybody this time, but watched the tops of the pines at the graveyard border where they swung in the wind and dipped.

"Where were you last Saturday night
While I was lying in jail?

> *Walking the streets with another man.*
> *I had no one to go my bail.''*

And whatever had been with me when I sang in the church house was with me still, the calm, strong voice that had stood by my side. Now while I was playing and singing so fast and hard, I recognized what it was. It was my own sadness, which had come out of my body and taken a shape apart from me. It was the ghost of the way things used to be, given to me to make it a little easier to keep on going down the road. I'd been wrong about it in the church house, because it wasn't going to go away. It was my own sorrow and would always be with me and I could call it to come whenever I wanted to sing. A ghost and my companion.

> *''Ain't going to work on the railroad,*
> *Ain't going to work on the farm.*
> *I'll hang around the shack*
> *Till the mail train comes back*
> *And roll in my sweet baby's arms.''*

When I finished, it seemed to me I'd finished with a great many things. Maybe I could sing like that whenever I wanted and maybe I would never sing again. I didn't care. A slow, wide feeling of peace settled in me like snow drifted over a new-plowed field; I didn't want anything to disturb it.

None of the people said anything, not even to one another. They started away and I waited for them to go, keeping my distance. Then I headed back to the church to pick up my guitar case.

But there at the gate the stranger with the shiny wristwatch and the black leather carrying case stopped me. "That was mighty fine singing," he said. "I don't know when I've been so impressed. You've got a wonderful voice, just wonderful."

"Thank you," I said, and tried to push on by him.

"Wait a minute." He stepped back to block my path. "My name is Ramey Bucke," he said, "and I'm a country-music promoter from Nashville, Tennessee. So when I tell somebody they've got a good voice, it means something. I don't travel up and down this country just for my health. You've got a good big old-fashioned voice and there might be some things we could do with it if we got you the right kind of material and some good handling and all."

"Much obliged," I said. "But I don't believe there's anything I need right now." I tried again to get past him.

"Just a minute," he said. "I was standing so far back there at the grave that I'm not sure I was able to record your song too well." He held out toward me a little wire-covered tube connected with a black cord to the carrying case. That was the first microphone I ever saw.

I looked down at it and then looked up at him, square in the face. "Mister," I told him, "if you don't get that fancy little machine out of the way, I'll bust it to a thousand pieces."

He stood aside then, and that was the end of it.

But of course that was not the end and only the beginning. If that was the end, you wouldn't be here, right?

I'm begging your pardon now for giving such an almighty long answer to a short and simple question. I know what I'm supposed to say. Ramey Bucke—who is my agent these days—told me last night that a woman from a music newspaper would be here this morning to interview me. So we tried to figure out some questions you might be asking and sure enough you hit on one: If I could have one single wish to come true, what would it be? Right over there in that desk drawer is a sheet of paper with the answer he wanted me to say: I wish for peace everywhere in the world.

It's a good answer, I reckon, but tremendous ambitious for a Horton County guitar picker. If you really did want to know, I'll tell you.

I wish I had never come to this damn crazy town of Nashville with its blinking lights and yellow-haired women and trashy money people. I wish I'd never heard myself coming out of a radio speaker or in a nightclub with no air or squeezed down on a record player. I wish I was back at the head of Big Sandy Cove in the Carolina hills at Caney Barham's house, me and him singing "Brokenhearted Lover" or any other old-time song you'd care to mention, and laughing till we were red in the face. Or if it couldn't be that way, if it happened that he was fated to die, then I wish I was on a grassy bald on the southern side of Ember Mountain, singing into the wind and the blue daylight, because nowhere else on the earth could he ever hear me now.

MISS PRUE

 Miss Prue had received news that her faithful suitor, Mr. M., had died a suicide, but still she waited in full confidence for his knock. He had taken a drug, they said. It would certainly be in his character to float off to eternity in a numb sleep. Suicide was very naughty, of course, but she had to admire his taste; no loud noises or bad smells, no ugly ropes or machines. He had just drifted away, as their conversation had so languidly drifted every Thursday afternoon for the past twenty years.

Was all in good order for their accustomed tea? The rug was swept, the furniture dusted and oiled, the windows sparkling. Her gray-barred emasculated cat, Wisdom, lay fat and sleeping on the hearth where the low fire licked. The doilies were in place, starched stiff. She had made beaten biscuits, and there were boiled ham and strawberry preserves. She took pride in meticulous order, decorous behavior. If anything got upset, if her plans went awry, what might happen? But nothing ever went wrong; she was too careful. Mr. M. would be pleased, as he always was.

One. Two. Three.

There they were, his habitual raps. They sounded muffled, weak, in the dim and motionless air of her drawing room. Before answering she examined herself in the heavy gilt-framed mirror that hung above the dark mahogany table. Her hair was gray now, but she had applied a modicum of color to her cheeks. The high-necked dress, color of a fallen oak leaf, set her face off, she thought, sufficiently.

She opened, and it was Mr. M. indeed, but changed. Death had transfigured this gentle man; he was thinner than ever, and pale, pale as a cloud, pale as a glass curtain. His eyes were like cinders in the deep sockets. He seemed to belong more to the cool gray autumn wind than to the world of animal flesh.

"Punctual as usual," she said brightly. "Do come in, Mr. M. May I take your coat?"

She waited as he struggled wearily out of the long, weighty overcoat. She didn't help, not wanting to touch the dead man. Never had she touched him when alive. She took the coat carefully when he offered it and hung it with his black muffler in the closet.

"Won't you sit in the fireside chair?" she asked. "It's a raw, cold day. The tea will be ready soon, and that should warm you."

"Thank you," he said. His voice was windblown ash in a desert land.

She went into her gleaming little kitchen and set the pot off the heat and spooned in the Earl Grey and covered the pot with a blue knit cozy. She took it into the drawing room and placed it on the hearth, as company for Wisdom. Then they sat and waited for it to brew.

She tried not to stare. "Well, here you are," she said.

"Yes."

"I knew you'd come, no matter what. It's Thursday afternoon."

It seemed to require great effort for him to turn his eyes toward her. "It is the last time, Miss Prue."

She clucked her tongue. "Now don't be downhearted, Mr. M. Into every life some rain must fall. We have to bear up, you know."

"But I died, Miss Prue. I ought really to be in my grave, awaiting judgment."

"Yet you came to call on me. It's so like you, so thoughtful."

"No," he said. "It isn't manners. Not exactly."

"Let us take our tea," she said. She poured two steaming leafy cups. He supported his saucered cup with one hand on his bony knee. When she brought her proud tray of food, he declined it with an exhausted wave of his hand.

What a pity, she thought. Poor man. "But you did come to call," she said. "For see, here you are."

"I had to ask a question."

"What do you wish to ask?"

"Was there something, was there anything, I could have said that—"

"That what? Please speak clearly, Mr. M."

"That would have made it different between us?"

"How can you desire it to be different? We have been a fixed pair these last twenty years."

"We might have been closer," he said, and what a world of cold this latter word implied.

"How closer? How steadier? Few married couples are as close and steady as we have been."

"Might we not have gotten married?"

She flicked her hand at the question as if it were a tedious housefly. "That is not in our personalities, I think. We are a different sort, you and I."

"So there was nothing I might have done?"

"Done? Oh yes, done. You might have swept me off my feet, Mr. M. You might have carried me away like an impetuous bandit or a dashing pirate."

His eyes dropped. But maybe he was not looking at the hooked rug, but through the crust of the earth to the shoals of mineral and the molten seas of fire. "That was not my style," he said at last.

"Oh no." She crowed her agreement. "Not *our* style. Not at all. We are well fitted, the two of us."

"That was the tragedy," he said.

"A melodramatic word, *tragedy*. Haven't we enjoyed our company together? Haven't we had our Thursdays, our tea and our talk?"

"There are other things." His voice was like the sound of wind in a ragged thornbush. "I know now that there are other things, though I don't quite know what they are."

"Then how do you know there are other things?"

"If there were not, I would be content in my death. I would be a long way from here, Miss Prue."

She rose abruptly. "You haven't touched your tea, and it is simply delicious. I shall take another cup, and some ham and preserves. I took the trouble, Mr. M., of beating biscuits."

Slowly he turned his head aside. "I'm sorry."

"Now now, don't fret." She poured her tea and returned to her seat. "I believe that you never learned to appreciate some very important things. We were never vulgar, but didn't you find our delicacy with one another actually . . . well, sensual? There were times when we positively *swilled* nuance. Was that lost upon you?"

"Lost?" It was the cry of the Arctic moon. "Everything is lost. There is nothing."

"Nonsense," she said firmly. "You have allowed this matter of your health to upset you unduly. I am going to brew a fresh pot, and you are to have some and see if it doesn't brace you up. I won't take no for an answer, Mr. M." When she lifted the pot from the hearth, Wisdom opened one yellow eye, then returned to his dream of Stilton cheese and scarab beetles.

In the kitchen she made tea afresh, humming an old sentimental song. She had seen him this way before, disheartened over one or another. But she'd brought him around. What the hapless man needed was a good talking-to, a pepping-up to stiffen his backbone. Men were so easily dis-

couraged. It was a bad thing, to let oneself get down like
that, and something she never allowed herself.

When the kettle whistled, she thought for a moment it
wailed her name. *Miss Prue Prue Prue.* She pursed her lips,
set the kettle off.

When she returned to the drawing room, it was as still
as an engraving in an old album. His cup and saucer were
on the marble-topped coffee table, but Mr. M. was absent.
She whispered, "Where are you?"

She looked in the closet. His overcoat and muffler were
not there. "Oh, Mr. M.," she said.

The cat opened his eyes and closed them again.

She looked out the front door. The light was gray, the
air cold. "I forgot to tell you about Wisdom," she said.
"Last week he had a strange infection, but I'm sure he's all
right now."

Mr. M. was not there; no one was there. A big crow
settled in the top of the oak by her flagstone walk. It gave
her one cool and careless regard, then flew off across the
valley and over the mountain.

MANKIND JOURNEYS
THROUGH FORESTS OF
SYMBOLS

1

There was a dream, and a gaudy big thing it was, too, and for six hours it had been blocking Highway 51 between Turkey Knob and Ember Forks. The deputies came out to have a look-see, tall tobacco-chewing mountain boys, and they stood and scratched their armpits and made highly unscientific observations like, "Well, I be dog, Hank," and "Ain't that something, Bill," and so on, you can just imagine. Finally Sheriff Balsam arrived with his twenty years of law-enforcement experience, but he, too, seemed at a loss.

The dream would measure about two stories tall and five hundred yards wide and it lay lengthwise on the highway for a distance of at least two miles. It was thick and goofy, in consistency something like cotton candy. Its predominant color was chartreuse, but this color was interlaced with coiling threads of bright scarlet and yellow and suffused in some areas with cloudy masses of mauve and ocher. It had first been reported about seven o'clock in the morning, but it had probably appeared earlier. Traffic was light on that stretch.

Sheriff Balsam observed that it would be a problem. No dream of such scale and density had been reported before in North Carolina, and this one looked to be difficult. Balsam had never dealt much with dreams, and there was a lot *to* this one. It was opaque and complex; you could see it working within itself like corn-whiskey mash in a copper cooker.

Balsam and the boys set up the blinking barricades down the highway, detouring the traffic onto a circuitous gravel road, and then there was nothing to do but wait. The theory was that when the dreamer woke, the dream would go away, disappear like a five-dollar bill in a poker game. And who could afford to lie in bed all day dreaming? Balsam and Hank and Bill returned to the sheriff's office in the Osgood County courthouse to busy themselves with lost dogs and traffic citations.

But by lunchtime the telephone began ringing and didn't let up. Folks were irate. Whose dream was it out there on the highway and what, by God, was Balsam going to do about it? "I voted for you last time, Elmo Balsam," said the vexed farm wife.

"I was the only one running, Ora Mae," Balsam said.

Finally he left the receiver off the hook and looked over at Hank and Bill, who were sharing a newspaper and a spittoon. "Boys," he said, "looks like we got bigger troubles than we thought."

"Yup," says Hank, and Bill says, "Looks like."

Balsam said, "What if whoever is dreaming that damn thing is drugged?"

Now there was a thought. Crazed drug freaks everywhere these days. Just think of the high school over there. Hank and Bill thought of the high school and shook their heads mournfully. *These days anymore, boy, you just don't know.*

"Might be quite a while before he comes out of it. And it could be even worse."

Worse brightened their interest considerably. They looked at Balsam in mute wonder.

"He might could be in a *coma*. Might be weeks and months. Might be years."

They looked at one another.

"I think we ought to get an expert up here from the State Office," Balsam said. He looked the number up and paused with his finger in the dial. "What do you boys think?"

Whew, Lordy, the State Office. Bill thought it over and said, "Yup," but you could tell he considered it an extraordinary step to take. Bill was the slow and earnest thinker. Hank, the ebullient enthusiast, was intoxicated by every whim that sailed down the pike.

They watched astonished as Balsam spoke into the telephone. They fully realized it was the State Office on the other end of the line.

Balsam hung up and told them that the State Office had already dispatched an expert; he ought to have been here by now. Seemed that a farmer flying over in his Cessna had spotted the dream and radioed the highway patrol and they'd gotten in touch with the State Office. The State Office had said a lot of other things to Balsam that they would of course regret saying later on, so he wouldn't repeat all that. But they were to keep an eye out for this expert, Dr. Litmouse his name was, who ought to have been here by now.

Just at that precise moment a state-patrol car pulled up in front of the sheriff's office, blue light twirling, siren whining. Two men entered. One was only a patrolman, but it was easy to see the other was an expert, the genuine article. His pinstripe gray suit was too large for him, as if he'd wandered into someone else's clothing by accident. He had but a paucity of hair and what there was was white and frazzly. The thick lenses of his spectacles so magnified his eyes, they looked like they were pasted on the glass. He was carrying a quart mason jar of brownish liquid.

"I'm Dr. Litmouse," he said. "I hope I'm not late."

Balsam rose with unaccustomed alacrity and shook his hand. Introductions all around.

"I guess you're anxious to get out on Fifty-one and see about that dream," the sheriff said. "We'll drive you out."

"Kind of you," Dr. Litmouse said. "I wonder if you have a safe place where I might store this." He held up his quart jar.

"Sure thing, Doc. What is it?"

"I suppose you might call it a kind of secret formula," the expert said.

Balsam gave the muddy liquid an uneasy look. "We'll put it in the safe. . . . No, better put it in the filing cabinet," he said, remembering that he'd forgotten the combination to the safe. It wasn't needed; Balsam and Bill and Hank were not often entrusted with secret formulae.

"Fine."

Balsam and Dr. Litmouse got into one car, Hank and Bill into another, and the patrolman followed them. Dr. Litmouse seemed preoccupied, saying not a word the whole trip. This guy wouldn't look like much if you saw him just anywhere, Balsam thought, but once you knew he was an expert . . . That was what Science would do for you. Balsam began to regret that he wasted his evenings watching championship wrestling on TV instead of reading chemistry books.

When they arrived at the famous dream, they found a little girl, a towhead about eight years old, standing just this side of it. She wore jeans and a blouse and was popping bubble gum.

Balsam hollered at her. "Hey, little girl. You get back away from that thing."

She snapped a bubble. "There's already three cars drove in there."

"Good Lord," he said. "Didn't they see the detour sign?"

"Sure they did," she said. "Drove right around it."

"They must be crazy."

"They didn't look crazy."

"Well, you stand back now."

Dr. Litmouse had already begun to examine the dream. He paced back about fifteen feet and surveyed it from there, then walked over and stared closely, like a man peeking through a keyhole. He pulled his earlobe, pushed his glasses up on the bridge of his nose. "Bring me my case out of the car, please," he said.

Hank fetched it.

"What do you think, Doc?" the sheriff asked.

"I'm not quite sure," he said. He set the case on the ground and squatted to open it. It was a large square box of black leather, lined with blue plush. Inside were flasks and bottles and test tubes, forceps, big hypodermics, clamps, and other unrecognizable stainless-steel instruments. He took out a two-liter beaker and a pair of shiny clamps and went back. He inserted the clamps gently into the surface of the dream and gave them a slight twist and slowly withdrew. A hand-sized blob of it came away like greenish cobweb, trailing filmy rags. The expert stuffed this blob into the beaker and held it up against the sunlight to judge whatever he was judging. He shook his head.

From his vest pocket he took a book of papers like cigarette papers except that they were blue and pink. He blew on them and tore out one of each color. He lowered the blue paper down into the dream blob and took it out and looked. Obviously dissatisfied, he threw it to the ground. Then he tried the pink paper.

Bill nudged Hank. *Damn, boy, look at him go.*

The stooped gray expert held the beaker to his face and sniffed—carefully. Then, very gingerly, he put his finger into it. When he brought his finger out, it was tinted pale green and dream threads clung to it. They watched, muscles tensed, as he put his finger into his mouth.

Almost immediately a fearful transformation came over the scientist. He trembled head to toe in his too-large suit like a butterfly trying to shed its cocoon. His eyes rolled crazily and blinked back, showing the wild whites. His voice was high and thin and visionary when he cried out:

> *"La Nature est un temple où de vivants piliers*
> *Laissent parfois sortir de confuses paroles;*
> *L'homme y passe à travers des forêts de symboles*
> *Qui l'observent avec des régards familiers."*

Then he keeled over flat on the ground, unconscious.

Balsam sprang into action. "Hank, Bill! Pick that man up and bring him over here. Hurry up. And stay away from that stuff, whatever it is."

Hank and Bill deposited Dr. Litmouse at the sheriff's feet, and he knelt to examine him. The doctor's eyelids quivered and he began to breathe more regularly, regaining his senses. He sat up and rubbed his face with both hands.

"You okay, Doc?" Balsam asked.

"I'll be all right in a moment," he said. He put his head between his knees and breathed deeply.

"You took a bad turn there. Had us all worried," Balsam said. "What is that stuff, anyhow?"

Dr. Litmouse rose and brushed ineffectually at his baggy suit. "It's a more serious problem than we thought. The mass we have to deal with here is not a dream but something rather more permanent. Unless we can think of a solution."

"What is it then?"

"I hate to tell you," Dr. Litmouse said, "but I believe it's a symbolist poem. I'd stake my professional reputation that it's a symbolist poem."

"You don't say," Balsam said.

Hank nudged Bill with his shoulder. *Damn-a-mighty, boy, symbolist poem. You ever see the beat?*

The little girl came over to stare at Dr. Litmouse and to pop a bubble at him. "What's the matter with you?" she asked. "You act like you're falling down drunk."

2

Dusk had come to the mountains like· a sewing machine crawling over an operating table, and Dr. Litmouse and

Hank and Bill and Balsam were back in the sheriff's office. Balsam sat at his desk, the telephone receiver still off the hook. Bill and Hank had resumed their corner chairs. The three lawmen were listening to the scientist's explanation.

"Basically it's the same problem as a dream, so it's mostly out of our hands. Somebody within a fifty-mile radius is ripe to write a symbolist poem but hasn't gotten around to it yet. As soon as she or he does, then it will go away, just as the usual dream obstructions vanish when the dreamers wake." He took off his glasses and polished them with his handkerchief. His eyes looked as little and bare as shirt buttons and made the others feel queasy. They were glad when he replaced his spectacles.

"It's worse than a dream, though, because we may be dealing with a subconscious poet. It may be that this person never writes poems in the normal course of his life. If this poem originated in the mind of someone who never thinks of writing, then I'm afraid your highway detour will have to be more or less permanent."

"Damn," Balsam said. He leaned back in his swivel chair. "What do you mean, more or less?"

"Death," replied the expert.

"Say what, Doc?"

"If it doesn't belong to a practicing poet, you may be stuck with it until the originator dies."

"Damn," Balsam said. "And there ain't nothing we can do? Nothing at all?"

"In Europe they've been heavily afflicted, but in America we've been lucky," Dr. Litmouse said. "The largest American symbolist obstruction is in California, and is, I would estimate, about twice the size of this one. Fortunately, it's at the bottom of a canyon in Whittier National Park and no real inconvenience. But it's been there, Sheriff Balsam, for fifteen years."

Hank and Bill exchanged glances. *Fifteen years, boy.*

Balsam said, "Doc, we can't leave that thing there fifteen years. That's an important road."

"I sympathize, but I don't know what can be done."

The sheriff picked up a ballpoint pen and began clicking it. "Well, let's see. . . . There it is, and it'll go away if somebody writes it down on paper."

"Correct."

"What we got to do then is get folks around here started writing poems. Maybe we'll hit on the right person."

"How will you do that?"

He bit the pen. "I don't know. . . . Bill, Hank—you boys got any bright ideas?"

They shook their heads sorrowfully. Bill spat; Hank spat.

"Say, Doc," Balsam said, "you tested this here, uh, poem. Did you get any notion what it was about?"

"Very difficult to say. It affects the nervous system powerfully, sending the victim into a sort of trance. Coming out of it, I remember no details. I have only impressions. I would say that the poem is informed by tenuous allusion, strong synesthesia, and a wide array of hermetic symbols. But it was quite confusing, and I could gather no details, no specifics."

"That's too bad," the sheriff said. "I was hoping we could track it down. Because if it was about Natural Bridge, say, and we could find someone who had been visiting up to Virginia . . ."

"It's a symbolist poem, Sheriff," Dr. Litmouse said. "Doesn't have to be autobiographical in the least. In this case, we're probably dealing with archetypes."

Hank winked at Bill. *We better watch out, boy. Them ole archetypes.*

"Well, what we got to do then is just get as many people as we can out there writing poems. Community effort. Maybe we'll luck out."

"How?" asked Dr. Litmouse.

He clicked his ballpoint furiously. He got a sheet of department stationery and began printing tall uncertain letters. The other three watched in suspense, breathing unevenly. When he finished, Balsam picked up the paper

and held it at arm's length to read. His lips moved slightly.
Then he showed them his work. "What do you think?" he
asked.

The SHERIFF'S DEPARTMENT
of OSGOOD COUNTY
in cooperation with the
NORTH CAROLINA STATE HIGHWAY DEPARTMENT
announces
A POETRY CONTEST
$50 FIRST PRIZE
Send entries to SHERIFF ELMO BALSAM
OSGOOD COUNTY COURTHOUSE
EMBER FORKS, N. C. 26816
SYMBOLISM PREFERRED!!!

"I suppose it's worth a try," Dr. Litmouse said, but he
sounded dubious.

3

Then opened the beneficent heavens and verses rained
upon the embattled keepers of the law.

Sheriff Balsam kept his equanimity. He had posted Collins, Dr. Litmouse's escort patrolman, out at the site to keep
an eye on the dream and report to the office. Collins radioed in every hour that there was no change.

The other four sat in the office, reading sheaf after sheaf
of manuscript. Dr. Litmouse held each page by a corner,
regarding every poem as if it were some new species of
maggot. Balsam turned pages mechanically; his eyes
looked tired. Hank and Bill read ponderously, chewing
their plugs as if they were digging graves.

Balsam glanced up. "Anything look promising?"

"These are just all Spring and Mother," Hank said. He
sounded aggrieved.

"How about you, Bill?" the sheriff asked.

"Kinda boring," he said. "Spring and Mother and all. But there was one—"

"What about it?"

"I thought it had something, but it didn't work out."

"Let's see it." Balsam squinted and read aloud. "'The bluebird in our firethorn tree Fills the merry day with glee. . . .' Aw, come on, Bill. This ain't the kind of thing we're looking for."

"Yeah, I know." He chewed. "But I was thinking if maybe it went different—"

"Different how?"

"Like if it wasn't no bluebird and glee and stuff. Like if it started off, 'The squalid eagle in the thornfire,' maybe we'd be on the right track."

Balsam gave him a steady gaze. "How you say that?"

"Say what?"

"'Squiggly eagle in the bush'?"

"I was trying to think how it might go. The squalid eagle in the thornfire . . . I guess I've got the whole wrong idea."

They looked at him with fierce interest.

Balsam turned to the expert. "What do you think, Doc?"

Dr. Litmouse nodded slowly. "It's worth a try. Why not?"

A sputter of static from the radio on the sheriff's desk and then the tinny voice of the patrolman. "Collins here, out at the site. You there, Sheriff Balsam?"

Balsam leaned and flipped a switch. "Right here," he said. "Anything happening out your way?"

"I think maybe I saw some movement. Top of it got a little ragged like maybe the wind took hold of it."

"When was this?"

"Just a minute ago. Nothing happening now, though."

"Stay right there and keep watch," the sheriff ordered. "I'll send some help." He cut the switch and stood up and took his keys out of his pocket. "Doc," he said, "you drive my car and radio back when you get there. When we hear from you, we'll start working with Bill here."

"Work with me how?" Bill's brow furrowed plaintively.

The sheriff led Bill to the desk and seated him. He crowded papers out of the way and got a fresh sheet and two pencils and laid them before the deputy. "You ever wrote any poems, Bill?"

He looked down at his big wrists. "Not much," he said. "Have you?"

His face and neck were scarlet. "Used to try one ever once in a while."

"I never knowed that!" Hank exclaimed. "Boss, I swear he never told me nothing about it."

"You're going to write one now, Bill," Balsam said.

"What do you want me to write?" He picked up a pencil as if it were loaded and cocked.

"Write it down about that squirrely eagle."

Bill wrote, sticking the tip of his tongue out of the corner of his mouth. "Now what?" he asked.

"Just go on from there," the sheriff ordered.

"I don't know nothing that comes next."

"You just settle down and see if it doesn't come to you."

"Come on, old hoss, you can do it!" Hank shouted.

Bill closed his eyes. His lips twitched. He opened his eyes and shook his head.

"Anything we can get to help you out?" the sheriff asked.

He thought. "Well, maybe, uh, maybe I could use a glass of wine?"

"Wine!" Hank was thunderstruck, but at a glance from Balsam recovered himself. "Damn right, good buddy. What you want? T-Bird? Irish Rose? Mad Dog?"

"Like maybe a pretty good burgundy," Bill said firmly.

"Hank, you zip down to the supermarket and see if they got any burgundy wine," the sheriff said. Hank started for the door, but Balsam halted him. "No. Hell. Wait. Get this boy the best champagne they got. Don't spare the horses."

"Damn right," Hank said, and went out.

Again the radio rattled and spoke. "Sheriff Balsam, this

is Dr. Litmouse. I'm in place out here at the site. We're ready to begin when you are."

Balsam switched on and said, "We're ready to go. We'll keep each other posted. . . . No, wait. Bill's going to be concentrating pretty heavy in here. Maybe we ought to stay off the radio for a while."

"Quite sensible," Dr. Litmouse said. "We'll wait for your call."

"Fine." The sheriff switched off and turned to Bill. "Don't worry about a thing," he said. "You just go on and write down your poem. Won't nobody disturb you."

"I don't know if I can," Bill said.

"Look here, Bill," Balsam said, "you're a deputy sheriff of Osgood County. I don't have to tell you what kind of responsibility that is. Sometimes the job is dirty and dangerous, but you knew that when you put on the badge. I never expect to see you back off from the job, boy. Never."

Bill swallowed hard. "Do the best I can," he said.

"Okay then. I'll be right over here in the corner. Anything you need, just holler. Don't forget we're all behind you one hundred percent." Balsam sat in a corner chair and pretended to read a sheaf of poems.

Bill lifted a pencil and laid it down again. He closed his eyes. His neck and shoulder muscles bunched and veins stood out in his temples. He breathed slow and harsh and a film of sweat covered his forehead.

He picked up the pencil and began to write, poking the tip of his tongue out of the corner of his mouth.

Hank came in with a bottle of champagne. He started to speak, but Balsam silenced him with a gesture. Hank looked at Bill with an expression of tender commiseration. He gave the bottle to the sheriff, who took it into the washroom and worked the cork out and poured a water tumbler full of the wine and took it to Bill, setting it gently on the desk.

Bill didn't notice. He scratched out old words and wrote in new ones. In a while he drained the glass without ap-

pearing to realize he'd done it. The expression on his face
was startling to look at.

Balsam and Hank sat watching Bill and glancing at one
another. Time seemed to stop.

Bill wrote and rewrote, grunting. At last, with a savage
anguished cry, he flung down the pencil and buried his
face in his hands. When he turned to Hank and Balsam,
his face was ashen and his brown hair had turned gray.
"That's all," he said. "I can't do no more. I can't."

They took his arms and half-dragged him to his usual
chair in the corner. "See how he is, Hank. We can have
an ambulance here in five minutes."

"I'll be all right," Bill said.

Balsam went to the radio. "Hey, Doc, are you there?
How's it look?"

The excitement of the scientist was unmistakable. "It's
all gone, Sheriff Balsam. Disappeared. You've done a fine
job back there."

"All cleared up?"

"Well, there are a few scattered patches, but the highway
is clear. No trouble. We can probably get rid of the leftovers
if Bill wants to correct his meter and line breaks."

"Hell with that," Balsam said. "Bill has done enough for
one day. You boys come on in." He clicked off and turned
to his deputies.

Hank was punching Bill's shoulder and wrestling him
about. "You hear that? You done it, old hoss! By damn,
you done it!"

Bill smiled weakly and tried to look modest.

"We ought to celebrate," the sheriff said. "What say we
finish off this here champagne?"

When Dr. Litmouse and Patrolman Collins came in, they
all switched to the corn whiskey Balsam kept in his bottom
drawer. They poured a couple of farewell drinks and talked
happily. Dr. Litmouse promised to turn in a glowing report
about the sheriff and his deputies to the State Office. They
shook hands and the other two departed. Patrolman Collins cut in the siren for a couple of blocks.

They listened, and then Balsam was struck by a memory. "Oh hell," he said.

"What's the matter?" Hank asked.

"The Secret Formula," he said. "The doc forgot his Secret Formula." He took it out of the filing cabinet and set it on his desk. They regarded it with apprehension.

"What do you reckon that stuff does?" Hank asked.

"I don't know," Balsam said.

"Well, hell," Bill said. "let's find out." He unscrewed the lid and stuck his finger into the liquid and tasted it.

Hank and the sheriff eyed one another. It was clear now that Bill had the courage of tigers; he was afraid of nothing.

"What is it?" the sheriff asked.

Bill licked his lips. "Barbecue sauce," he said. He thought for a moment, tasting. "With about a cup and a half of Château Beychevelle '78."

ALMA

 I feel different about women than a lot of men do
and I'll tell you why. It's because I had me my own woman
one time. I lived real close with her and that has made me
think thoughts apart.

The way it come about was there was a drover who told
me he had journeyed up from the marshlands and he was
pushing a string of twelve of them through the Suffering
Mountain foothills. Headed for Fort Ox 1, the soldiers
there, he said and I tell you exactly what he said because
I don't know better. But whatever he said is probably not
in sight distance of the truth. If you know drovers, you
know what I mean. I don't like them and never did.

Anyhow, they come to the edge of my campground there
at Busted River about five hundred yards down from the
big waterfall. He stopped them at the edge and I had to
think it was the plumb sorriest string of women ever I
laid eyes on. Most of them wouldn't make good buzzard
bait when he got hold of them and he had took no pains

to keep them up, never washing them down and hadn't put clothes on them and I could tell they'd been fed scanty, their ribs sticking out. The rattiest bunch you could think of, mud and dust and scabs and their hair all ropy and their eyes wild. There was some of them sick, I could tell by looking.

He had them strung together with some old moldy leather tack and he tethered them to a big shagbark hickory and come on in toward me with his hands up and open. Which meant he was all alone except for his livestock but didn't know whether I was alone or not. I was because I didn't journey with gangs no longer. I was fed up with the squabbles and the knife fights and the pizen cooking and I had struck out on my lonesome to fish and trap and hunt and never regretted it, though you got to keep on your toes every minute when you do that, being your only own protection.

Come toward me hands open and careful like I say and says to me, "Stand easy now. My name is Dingo and I'd like to rest a spell with you and maybe use your cooking fire."

"You alone?" I asked him.

"Not exactly," he said, and grinned a sideways grin.

"I don't mean the women."

"It's just me and the shoat line," he says, shoats being what some drovers call women. "But they won't be no trouble. I can stake them out in the woods. I'll move them downwind if the smell bothers you. I've got kind of used to it myself."

I thought for a minute but was pretty sure he was alone. If he'd been trying to spring something on me, he wouldn't've put his livestock at risk.

"All right then," I said. "Make you welcome. I've got my fire and there's a path to the river and that's all the camp I've struck here. If it will do you any good, make you welcome."

"A lot of good," he said, "and I thank you. First thing

for me is to take care of these shoats. Where'd you say that path was?''

I showed where and he gave them a hand sign and the women unshucked the tote sacks from their shoulders and laid them on the ground and I could see how glad they was to do it. Then he herded them off the way I pointed, taking them down to the river to drink.

While they was gone, I slipped away from the fire and made me a quiet circuit of my ground, trying to find any sign of others. I was pretty well satisfied already that he wasn't with no gang, but you can't be too careful up there in the mountain territories.

By the time he got back from the river I had some coffee going, parched oat coffee that was, and I was right tired of it after two months on the trail. He settled the women down by a blackberry thicket, downwind like he said, and staked them. Then he passed out some jerky and old biscuit amongst them. They would have to be watered again after that meal, I thought, but right then they seemed pleased to get something to eat.

So then he came over to where I was and I pointed to the coffee and he took some in a little tin cup he'd fetched along. He offered me a crumb of chew tobacco but I didn't take, not wanting to get too friendly in a hurry. You never know. But he was a free-talking jasper and said he was heading up to the fort to get shed of his women. Hoping to trade for firearms and ammunition or maybe for cutlery and if he couldn't get any of that, then just for canvas and cloth goods. "I don't much care what they bring, as long as I don't have to drive them no farther," he said.

I asked how long they'd been on the trail and he said ten days, which I judged a lie because those women had been marched a lot longer than that, easy to see. I just nodded, though, and figured to myself that this one was a raider. He had probably cut this string from one of the big herds heading south toward the Pleasure Cities. Snaked them away in dead of night and had to run them hard in

the dark and that was why they looked so bad. Either that
or he had come across some small outfit up on one of the
tributary trails and killed them and took the women and
made tracks out of there. Because he wouldn't be driving
them all alone if he wasn't running scared.

I asked him if Fort Ox 1 was a pretty fair market for
women and he said he hoped so. "If there hadn't been too
many drovers there before me," he says, and clawed in his
beard for a flea and was disappointed. "It kind of depends
on the weather. If it's good traveling then a pretty many
drovers will come through. But raining like it's been doing
and not so many. They'll probably take them no matter
because it's wonderful how many women the soldiers use
up. Use them for domestics, you know, swabbing and
scouring and whatnot and the way they treat their women
they don't last all that long." He drawled out that word
whatnot and slipped me a slow wink but I gave no sign.
None of my business what the soldiers do as long as they
don't conscript me, which they'd tried twice.

So the time wore on like that, us jawing, him mostly. He
asked me if I'd seen any other drovers in these parts and I
told him I'd seen a string of horses and then five days ago
a string of pigs, both headed south.

"No," he said, "I mean shoat lines. You see any drovers
with women come along this way?"

"You're the first I know of," I said.

He nodded and it was plain he was relieved and started
talking again. "It ain't much of a business," he says, "and
if I hadn't lit on such a long run of bad luck I'd never be
in it. Women, you couldn't dream what trouble and them
a glut on the market these days. They'll run a man crazy if
he don't keep a tight rein, so I made up my mind right
from the start I would. Dirty, you can see how dirty. And
you can't teach them nothing; it's like they ain't got nothing to learn with. Dangerous, too."

"I heard that," I said but they didn't look dangerous to
me, only miserable as dug-up moles. They had pushed

back the vines a little and huddled on the ground, picking twigs and trash out of each other's hair, picking off vermin. They were dog-weary and hollow-eyed and they would hug one another and croon and rock back and forth on their hams.

"Oh yeah. They'll jump a man in a minute if he was to get careless. And you wouldn't never want one of them to bite you, you know why?"

"Why is that?"

"Pizen," he said, and wagged his head slow. "A burning thirst comes over you and you swell up like a bullfrog."

I'd heard that and never believed it before and didn't believe it now. Because a body pretty often bites hisself by accident, his lip or inside his cheek. If it was so, the women would've died out long ago. "I've heard tell there's some people that raise them for food," I said. "I wouldn't want to eat nothing that would pizen me."

He leaned back against a stump and sipped off the rest of his coffee. "I've et I reckon just about everything," he says. "Dog and snake and I don't know what all. But I can't think how starved I'd have to get before I'd eat a woman. They're my trade, you see, so I know how dirty they are. I wouldn't eat one but I've heard that some do, like you say. You ever have much truck with women?"

"No," I said.

"Maybe you might want to learn a little. Come on over and I'll show you how a drover judges them to trade."

"I can see fine from where I'm at."

He stood up. "Come over and get you a good look so you'll see what I'm talking about."

We went over and he made them stand up and we passed down the line. I couldn't see much difference up close because I ain't much judge. The truth is, I never did really hold with woman trading. I know it's how things are and I suppose somebody will always be doing it but not me, never. Something ugly about the whole thing, the way they look at you dog-eyed but also in a way so you know there is something going on in their heads and you'll never know what. And other reasons, too, I had no words for then.

He tried to explain me the finer points of his stock and I made like I understood what he was talking about. But there was one of them that stood out from the others. She was a redhead or would be if she was washed up and she was a little bit smaller than the other women but wiry and looked to be quicker and maybe tougher. It was the way she carried herself, though, that made me take notice. She had been kicked and whipped but she wasn't *beaten*, if you know what I mean. The way she held her chin up, the way her eyes were bright and no dog in them. She might just step up and spit in your eye and say, "Do your damn worst and I'll endure it." She wasn't no cleaner than the rest of them and she must have been just as tired but she was different. One look at her and I knew and I wondered if Dingo knew.

"Well, what do you think of them?" he asked me.

"I guess they're fine," I said. "I ain't no hand at judging women."

"See any of them you might like to trade for?"

"In the first place I wouldn't know what to do with one and in the second place I ain't got nothing to trade with."

"You got you your mule there and your cart. I'll make you a square deal. You won't find nobody fairer than me."

"No thanks," I said. "I got to have my mule and cart. Especially this winter when I set up trapping. But I don't have no use for a woman."

He grinned that ugly little grin. "You would be surprised. Once you get a woman broke in good and get used to having her around, you'll wonder how you ever got along without."

All that meant to me was that I better not get accustomed. "Well, maybe next spring I might be interested," I says, "if I have a good season with my traps." Because I was set in my mind I'd never see him again.

"You don't know what you're missing, what a comfort
and ease one of these shoats can be to a man. Don't go by
the way you see them now. You get one of them cleaned
and fattened up a little and it makes a difference you can't
hardly picture."

"How could I get one fattened up? Here in these skinny
old hills I can just barely feed myself." I turned away and
went back to the fire. He come along with me and kept
talking trade but must've known I was having none.

Twilight was in the woods now and I went down to the
river and brought back some water and then fed my mule
Warlock a double handful of grain. Dingo had already put
more wood on the fire, so we commenced putting our grub
together to boil up a stew. He had some cornmeal and sea-
sonings and so he took some water and patted out john-
nycakes and slapped them on a sheet of tin by the fire. He
made sixteen of them and said there would be one apiece
for his shoats and two apiece for me and him.

"We could pass around some stew," I says. "We've got
enough for all of them."

"No," he said. "They've had jerky and hardtack and now
this johnnycake and in a little while I'll take them down
and water them again. If you overfeed them they get too
feisty. They get treacherous and then there's no telling. The
way I do is to keep their feed down during the drives and
then right before I'm ready to trade I fatten them up real
smart."

He went on about it, telling how he fixed them up to
sell, scrubbing them down and grooming them. Every one
of them carried her a dress in her tote sack along with some
other stuff they liked to have and when she was ready to
be sold she would put on her dress and it fetched up her
price something remarkable. No other time would she wear
it, especially not on the drive to get tore up and dirty. They
would comb out one another's hair and brighten their teeth
with sassafras bark and wash up all shiny and put on the

dresses and bring almost the same price as a good sound
horse. You had to be careful, though, about the dresses because they got a little wild then. Many a time they'd kill
for another's dress.

I was plumb sick of hearing about the woman trade.

It was night now and we ate the stew, which was better
than I was used to, and set by the fire misinforming each
other while trying to get some straight information and I'd
call it a draw. He was as stingy with the truth as a horse
trader about the years on his animals, but I'd got the measure of him and matched him lie for lie.

In a little while I was ready to bed down but he took
one last turn to look after his shoats. He unhitched the
women two by two and pegged them around the neck with
rawhide cord and led them off into the woods to shit.

I bided my time, laying on my blanket and just resting till
he got his business all took care of and laid hisself down. I
wasn't fool enough to go to sleep first and I made sure my
big knife was handy under my bedroll. I kept as still as a
blacksnake in the noontime sun till I heard him breathing
deep and easy and then my eyes got scratchy and I drifted
off with the sound in my head of the women moaning in
the dark.

I woke up with a jerk, thinking a long-legged bug had
crawled into my ear and it took me a minute to figure
things out. Of course, I'd already reached and had my knife
out and so I found that I was holding it pointed and ready
to use under the chin of that redheaded green-eyed woman
who had been tickling in my ear with a grass blade.

She didn't flinch and didn't drop her eyes, so we stayed
a long minute at stalemate, but I meant business. If she
made a quick motion, I would've cut her throat.

Finally I let my hand drop back, though I still kept the
knife ready, and then real slow she raised her hand to her
mouth and signed for me to be quiet. Then she leaned to-

ward me and scrooched down and put her face next to my ear, making sure I saw she kept her hands away where she couldn't do me no harm.

"My name is Alma," she says to me, whispering.

I was thunderstruck. I didn't have the least idea that women could even talk, much less have names. And then the notion that they might know what their names were was queer. I didn't do nothing but gape for a while and Alma settled back to wait me out. Because she must have figured it was going to take me some little time to catch on.

I raised halfway up on my elbows and she motioned me to keep quiet and lay down again. She looked over to where Dingo was stretched out by the fire and he wasn't stirring.

"What is it you want?" I said and I whispered, too.

"You can kill him," she said.

"Kill who?"

"Dingo," she said. "You can kill Dingo and then all of us would be yours. We would rather be your women than hisn."

"How come?"

"Because you're the better man. We would be your women and treat you sweet and act right. We wouldn't give you no trouble like we do Dingo."

"How did you get loose?"

"It ain't hard. I could get loose anytime except there wasn't no reason to till you showed up."

"I can't kill him," I told her. "And I ain't got no use for women."

"You could trade."

"I wouldn't trade women. That ain't my way."

"Don't need to kill him then," she said. "We can just tie him down. By the time he was to get loose, we'd be a long way gone."

"Then he'd track me down and do me in."

"Never," she said. "Not ever. He's a-scared of you, you being the better man."

I kept glancing over at Dingo because the talk with Alma had got a little heated, but he didn't move except to wiggle for comfort now and again, which is a sign that a person is asleep good and sound.

And she kept on after me. "I believe you're going to do it," she says. "I can tell you want to."

"It's just that I ain't got no use for women," I said.

"When you say that it means you never had one." She leaned her face next to mine and her eyes shone in the firelight and looked into me. Then she laid hold of me there for a minute where women do, though I didn't know that yet, and I looked away. "You're going to do it, I can tell you are." And rubbed me a little and then I decided I would.

Maybe it was just her looking at me like that and then laying hold of me. But more likely it was her talking in the first place. I couldn't get used to it and was confused. A lot of new notions had come too fast. So I thought that maybe if I'd been wrong about a few things before now, I might be wrong about a lot of things.

But the truth is, I didn't think it out all that close. I just decided I would throw in with her rather than with Dingo because I didn't like him and I didn't like women traders in general. They were not his women anyhow, not till he'd robbed some other trader. So I figured he was only getting paid back even, if I figured on it at all.

The hardest part was crawling over to him without waking him up. You never notice how loud you breathe till you have to breathe quiet and then you sound like you're heaving like a cantered horse? But I crawled on my belly the last few yards, moving pebbles out of the way so they wouldn't scrub and click.

I grabbed his blanket and rolled him over in a flash and felt under him for a knife or pistol. He was laying on his back and when I saw his foot come halfway up I pinned it with my knee and slipped the little dirk out of his boot and flung it into the fire. I didn't want Alma to get it and decide to do me after I'd done for Dingo. I didn't trust him, that would take a long time.

He was right strong, the twisty wiry type, but I outweighed him by a good thirty pounds and about all he could soon do was thrash and swear. I took care to pin down his hands because I knew he'd have another weapon or two on him somewhere, so I knelt on his chest, moving up, and was surprised to see that Alma held down his ankles to help me out. That showed a lot of gumption.

"Just settle down," I said, but that only made him thrash harder and swear meaner. "No now, you settle," I told him again. "I wouldn't want to have to hit you with a stick or rock."

So then he laid quiet but was still cussing in a low voice and I just let him work off his fury. Then when Alma handed me some rawhide thong she'd got from his gear, I tied his wrists first and then tied his feet to his neck with that Rag Mountain strangle knot the old-timers use. That one will take the fight out of anybody, but I couldn't let it stay on too long or he would straighten his legs out and choke hisself to death.

He looked a lightning bolt at me, spitting and groaning. "She's got you now, Fretlaw," he said. "You don't have the first notion what you've let yourself in for."

Alma got a handful of gravel and stuffed it in his mouth and then some dirt and leaves. She stepped on his cheekbone and ground her heel down.

"That's enough," I said.

"No," she says, "it ain't enough."

"Back off," I told her. "Unless you want to settle with me right now who'll be giving the orders."

She gave him a last kick but not so hard and said no settlement needed, I'd be the one giving the orders. "You don't never need to worry you won't be the boss," she said. Then she bent over him and fetched hold of a twine around his neck and jerked it loose and a little bone-handle double-edge knife come with it, which she handed over to me.

The women were all awake and they cowered back, mumbling and moaning and looking at us with eyes scared wild. When I made a step toward them, they all shifted back toward the blackberry thicket into the thorns.

"What about them?" I said.

"You ain't no trader. Why not turn them loose?"

"Is that what you want me to do?"

"Yes."

"They'll starve to death out here. Or worse."

"They've got their tote sacks," she says. "And anyhow, if it comes to that, they'd rather starve than be drove and sold."

"All right then," I told her, "turn them loose. But if they start to come at me, I'll kill all I can."

"You've got everything all wrong. They wouldn't never hurt you. You're the one that has saved them."

But Dingo spoke up to say, "If I was you, Fretlaw, I wouldn't sleep for a year. They're just waiting to cut your throat." It was hard to make out his words, Alma's dirt still in his mouth.

But they earned him anyhow another kick from Alma as she went by on her way over to untie the women. Then she stood talking to them in a low voice and I couldn't hear her. They were happy, laughing and crying and hugging and kissing on the mouth. A few of them glanced at me and nodded while Alma was talking, but most wouldn't look my way. Then they detached into couples and struck off into the woods.

Dingo glared at me. "You got to turn me loose," he says. "Them shoats will come back to murder me the first minute you're gone."

"I'm going to undo the strangle knot and tie your feet kind of loose. You'll be able to get free in just a little while. But if you come after me, I'll leave you to the mercies of my woman."

"That one woman will be your first thing to wish you never had."

I fixed his binding like I told him I would and he stretched out his legs and eased a little. "You might be right," I said, "but if you come after us, she'll be the first thing you wish you never owned, either."

He swore some more and began struggling with his bonds.

"Wait now," I said. "Wait till we're out of sight or I'll have to tighten them up again."

Alma came back to where I was standing over him. "Go set down," she said, "and rest easy. I'll get us ready to move out; you don't need to raise a hand."

And so she done it, scouring out the cookware with sand and a bucket of water and piling that and the bedrolls in the cart and packing Dingo's roll, too, without even a remark. I was dumbstruck again to see her hitch Warlock to the cart. Where could she have learned?

When we were all fixed to go, I climbed up on the seat board and took the reins, but nothing would do for Dingo except to holler out that I'd be sorry, and I said, "I'll take my chances," and clucked Warlock up and we headed out toward the old Deer Salt Trail. I knew we'd better keep pointed toward the deeper mountains and put some rough distance between us and this campground.

When we had rolled and bobbed along about two miles, I told Alma that Dingo wouldn't starve, that I had tied him up in a way so he could work loose in a little while.

"No, he won't starve," she says. "That's one thing a dead man don't worry about."

"What do you mean?" I asked her.

"They went back and got him."

"The women?"

"Yes."

"What about me? Will they be coming after me now?"

"Not while you're with me," she said. "So you better stick by me for a good long time."

I didn't say nothing and she could see I was feeling gloomy about Dingo and wondering what I'd let myself in for, so she gave a little laugh and spoke soft. "Just wait till we come to a stream tomorrow. I'll clean up good and wash my hair and get nice and shiny. I'll put on my dress I've got in my tote sack. You won't believe your eyes to see me in my dress. And you won't never be sorry we throwed in together, you'll see." And she rubbed me there again where she rubbed before, where it was a pleasure, and we went on in the dark.

She was right about a lot of things, Alma was. We put in the winter trapping up on the Swagback and come spring we went down to Two River Post and traded our pelts, wild dog mostly and some fox and right much beaver and musk-rat. She told me the kind of things to say when I traded with One-Eye Narbo there and played dumb herself and we come out all right.

That summer we just laid by the Upper Barrelhead and fished and loafed. Then with fall coming on she said we ought to head even farther north than the Swagback, all the way up to Frozenever, where hardly anybody had been. She said we'd do good there and we did.

Five years we put in together like that and prospered. Maybe things got too easy for us and that made her rest-less, I don't know. Because one day she asked me if I'd ever thought we might want a child.

I said no, I had never gave it a thought.

"Well, think about it," she says. "One day you and me, we won't be so young anymore. It would be a big help to have us a youngun."

"Let me ponder," I told her and I did. It's hard to picture yourself getting old and helpless and feeble, but that was what was coming if a flood or a rock slide or the rabies didn't carry us off first. Trouble was, I didn't know how to get hold of a youngun or what you did when you got one.

"That part's mostly up to me," she says. "The youngun is the woman's chore."

"What is it that you do?"

"Well, there's some things you and me do together." She chuckled and said, "You'll like that part. Then I have to go off by myself for a while and then if everything turns out all right, I come back with a child."

"Where do you go to," I asked, "that I can't go?"

"Where I go to it's all women and they kill any man that tries to get close. There's an island in the middle of Weeping Lake and the women there ferry me over and after a while I get to have a youngun to raise up and bring back to you."

"How long will you be gone?"

She frowned a little. "Hard to say. Maybe five years."

"No," I said in a hurry. "Five years. No."

"You don't know how chancy they are, little like that. If I was to bring back one that was too small, it might die up here in the woods. It's a hard way of life on a child."

"Bring back a big one," I says. "Get us a big old tough boy."

"All the ones you can get are only little."

"Well, I'll think," I said, "but I ain't much in favor."

That was only the beginning and the days went by and she kept talking till finally she talked me into agreeing as I halfway knew she would from the start. So we did the things we needed to do together and she was right about me liking that part of it. Then a few days after, we headed out to Weeping Lake and she got down from the cart there on the shore and we waited. In a little while we could see the ferryboat coming, the wind in its big black sails and the oars rowing, the black boat scuttering across the lake like a water beetle.

"Leave now," Alma told me. "Don't wait till the Guardian Women get here. They're well armed and they don't like men. So you go on and come back three springs from now at shadblow time. Like we said we'd do."

"I've changed my mind," I said. "We don't need no child. Let's go back to the mountains where it's been good for us."

"No now," she says. "We've done decided and you won't turn on your word, Fretlaw. I know you."

"You could change your mind, too."

"This is the chance we need to take. And if it turns out right, everything with us will be better than now and for a long time to come."

"Well, I won't turn on my word," I said. "But it don't feel right to me. My heart misgives me about this."

"It'll turn out fine," she says, and put her arms around me for a big warm hug. "Now go on."

So I did like she said. At the top of the sand ridge I stopped Warlock so I could square around and look at her standing there at the shore of the lake with the big black boat bearing down on her. I could see some of the Guardian Women on board in armor and with spears and pistols and cutlasses, but mostly I looked at Alma, how small she seemed all of a sudden with the big boat in front of her and all the width of Weeping Lake around. And it come to me then that she was scared, too, just as scared as I was, and I felt a little bit proud, too, as well as scared and sad.

And that was the last I ever saw of her, her alone like that, with the boat coming on. I went back the next spring and every shadblow for eight years now I go down to the shore of the lake and wait for as many weeks as I can stand it.

I'm not alone, neither. Every now and then there's another man or two will be there waiting, but the boat don't come for them no more than it does for me. I suggested one time that we ought to get our own boat and head out to the island and bring our women back and one of them, Benthook it was, says to me, "That's been tried before and the Guardians sink them every time. There's many a good man drownded in Weeping Lake."

I still might do it, though. I'm going to wait this springtime on the shore and maybe the next, but if Alma don't show up I'm going out on the lake and search for that island.

Whenever I hear them talking in the whiskey sheds about women, going on about how dirty they are and how they're pizen and more murderous than bobcats and copperheads, I just feel weary in my bones. Because I had me a woman one time, my own woman, and I know different. And if I run across any traders in the mountains running shoat lines, I'm going to try to find how to get those women away and turn them loose.

AFTER REVELATION

1

 Then one evening I woke from a nap to find the door of my cell open and I walked out. Simple as that. The other cells were empty and the compound was empty and the big gate flung wide. I walked out of the deserted stockade, no one to stop me.

I'd been sentenced for practicing science. Our customary history has it that civilization twice destroyed itself by means of science, and they were going to prevent my doing it to them again. So they hauled me up on charges and tried me, what a farce.

This was the village council. I had known every one of the old buzzards since I was a child, and they knew me, too. They didn't scare me. The last new thought that any of them ever had was the discovery that girls are different from boys—and most of them were too old to remember that one.

"What is science?" I said. "You tell me what science is and I'll tell you whether I've been practicing it or not. Then we can all go home."

"Now, George, you know what it is as well as we do. The council is not going to waste its time quibbling over terms. We all realize how clever you are with words." This was Stavros, the council elder. He spent a lot of his valuable time trying to look the part of a sage. Long white hair cut severely at the shoulders, a grave expression on his wrinkled face, measured speech—maybe he deceived a few backward adolescents. Nobody else.

"Tell you what," I said. "I'll go down to the stockade and turn myself in. The council can stay here and formulate a definition of science. When you finish that little job, come and get me. Then we'll have a trial."

"Now wait, George," Stavros said. "There are procedures—"

"Goodbye, geniuses," I said, and stalked out of the chamber.

During this time I was smitten with the widow Larilla. I used to sit holding her hands in mine and gazing into her lovely brown eyes by the hour. I wrote bad canzones in praise of her midnight-colored hair and her gull-wing eyebrows. So I went by her house to tell her I was headed to jail, but she wasn't home. I left a note.

At the stockade I told Bert, the gatekeep, to let me in. "I'm a dangerous bad man, Bert. You'd better put me away. I'm out to destroy civilization."

"Again?" he said. "What have you been doing, George?"

"Practicing science," I said. "Do you know what kind of crime that is?"

"No."

"Well, in my case it amounts to collecting wildflowers."

"Oh," he said, with a careful lack of interest.

"Anybody else put away here?"

"Croya's here. Charged with black magic."

"That means she's been peddling her aphrodisiacs again. You ever try any of her potions, Bert?"

"No."

"Well, don't bother," I said. "They don't work."

He took me to a cell and I went in and stayed three days. I was going to stay there forever if I had to. The council was either going to apologize or they were going to try me publicly. In order to try me, the old geezers would have to define science, and I was looking forward eagerly to hearing that marvel of intellectual endeavor.

2

But then I woke to find my cell door open, the stockade deserted, and I came out. Everything had changed in three days. The village had changed; the whole world was different from what it had been before.

I knew something had happened, but I didn't know what. I could feel the changes in the air about me and it seemed there were different smells; all sorts of sensations I had never felt before.

For one thing, there were few people in the village. It was just at that late twilight hour when we first light the lamps, but now only twelve scattered lights shone in the houses. And no last excited shouts of children before they are ordered in at night, and no stir and mutter of preparing meals. No dogs barking. Only four lonesome smokes out of the chimneys.

The tavern was closed but Sylvia sat on the bench in front of it, her guitar across her lap. Sylvia is the village's blind ballad singer. Long gray-blond hair down to her waist, clear blue sightless eyes. A wicked way with her songs. I'd once paid her handsomely to stop singing her scurrilous ballad about Larilla and me. Then I realized how fine a song it was and felt I missed hearing it and had to pay her again to sing it anew.

"Good evening, Sylvia," I said.

"George?" A voice like the tingling of spider-thread.

"It's me. What's been going on? Everything seems different."

"Everything *is* different."

"Well, tell me about it, please. I haven't heard anything. I've been in jail. Do you want to know why I was in jail?"

"You haven't heard anything?"

"Not a thing," I said, a bit miffed that she wasn't interested in my story.

"The Owners have arrived," she said.

"What Owners?"

"The people that own men."

"What men?"

"Mankind," she said. "The people that own the human race."

"I didn't know that anybody owned the human race."

"None of us knew," she said. Her voice became more intimate, more silvery; she might have been talking to herself. "But hadn't you always wished that somebody did? Hadn't you hoped that there was someone who knew how to take care of you?"

Well . . . no. Maybe back in the furthest reaches of my mind I'd entertained this wistful fancy, but I'd never thought about it directly. Now that I did, the notion was as repulsive as it was attractive. In the first place, why would anyone want to own that tedious, quarrelsome rodent, mankind? "I don't know," I said.

"Now they've arrived," she said. "That makes it all different. Everything."

"Where did they come from?"

"Down from the sky, some say. Others say they came up out of the rivers."

"Nobody knows, then."

"Nobody knows much of anything."

"How do we know they own us?"

"Because that's something you don't mistake," she said. "That fact was clear as soon as they showed up. You'll know it, too, George. You like troublesome questions; you like to make fun of what people believe. But this is simple truth."

"It doesn't sound simple. Anything but. And where," I asked, "is everybody? The village is almost empty."

"They went north, south, east, and west," she said. "Following rumors, making pilgrimages."

I could believe that. When people are faced with new situations, they run around in circles. "What about you?" I asked. "Why are you sitting here in front of the tavern?"

"I'm waiting for an Owner to come," she said. "Then I'll know what to do."

"You're just going to sit here by yourself? It's getting dark, Sylvia."

"Yes, George, it's getting dark. I'm blind, I'm not stupid."

"Do you want me to leave you sitting here?"

"Yes," she said.

3

I went to Larilla's house, and there I saw one of the Owners.

The only light was in her bedroom, so I stepped round to the back of the house and peeped in at the window. Larilla was sitting before her mirror, brushing out her lovely long black hair. She crooned a little melody as she brushed and it tugged at my heart. I'd heard it a hundred times; often I heard it in memory when I was away from her. Does this detail say something about my passion for Larilla? After we met, I never saw the hour I didn't think of her.

The Owner was seated in a chair in a corner, watching her. He watched with a delicate but keen interest the long, leisurely strokes and the hair sifting down in skeins as the brush let go.

Sylvia was right. Easy to know that here was a personage who deserved to own mankind, if that was his desire. There was about him a full but unimposing awareness and a deep, whole calm. I felt certain as I looked through the window that he knew of my presence there, that the fact of my presence interested him as much as Larilla did, and that he was prepared to acknowledge me and understand. He possessed a serenity so profound and secure that it could not even be described as benevolent; benevolence would be an accidental quality of his personality.

He was a tall man; even sitting down he looked to be imperially tall. His features were grandly straightforward: a wide forehead under his ivory-blond hair, a fine straight nose, and large gray eyes as clear and cool as water. He wore a plain gray tunic and white linen trousers and sandals. Now it seems to me that except for his height there was little extraordinary in his physical appearance. But the attitude in which he held his body—easy, open, willing, and yet dignified—invited respect. And the poised, attentive attitude of his mind imposed deference, but without seeming to impose.

In short, he was epitome of what an Owner should be, and what I suppose the Owners are, though he is the only one I have seen as yet.

The Owners are, I believe, those who can pay full attention to someone else.

I withdrew from the window and walked in the road, heartsick. I wasn't jealous; that was too silly. The world was changed entirely; jealousy was one of those dispositions, like greed, that had no place anymore. I looked in myself for jealousy and found only longing, an intense longing to be near an Owner who would give me his calm attention, who would shed that broad and deep serenity over my troubles, who would bring peace the way a lamp brings a warm and pleasant glow into a dark room.

It had come to me, as I looked in the bedroom window, that there must be a single Owner for each person. That seemed right, inevitable; and it explained why the villagers had departed. Each was looking for his Owner—except for those few like Sylvia who were waiting for an Owner to come to them.

I found that I could not wait. Perhaps no one would come for me. I was stricken with grievous longing and driven on the roads under the starry night. I, too, must leave and go as a pilgrim; and even as I realized that fact and began to see a little of what lay before me, I thought, Wherever I roam tonight I shall see the slow strokes of Larilla's brush and hear her little song.

I walked to the edge of the village and looked back. I could see it all in my mind: the warm sleepers and the many empty beds, the clothes hanging on pegs, the shoes and chamber pots beneath the beds. I could see the dying coals in the ovens and the meats and vegetables and spices in the jars. I could smell the fatty oil lamps burning and the mouse droppings inside the walls and the gray cat's fur where it napped in the ingle.

My village has been like a nest of little birds waiting to learn to fly, I thought, and I walked away from it then. Midnight moved beside me on the road, a silent companion walker, and a yellow star on my left-hand side kept winking a message, but I could not make out the meaning.

4

I had not gone a mile or so before I saw firelight fitful behind the brush and trees beside the road. I slipped down off the road and toward the light, toward a mutter of elder voices. I hid in the bushes at the edge of a small clearing and peeped, to see what I could see.

Who should it be but the village council out in the midnight woods? The old ones stood warming themselves by the fire and talking. I felt a twinge of pity for them. When things were normal, this council had been an ignorant and helpless bunch of fools. Now that everything had changed, now that the Owners had arrived, they must feel perfectly useless, without hope or purpose. What was the point of a village council when there was no longer a village?

Old Stavros asked the questions for all of them. He paced in the firelight, rubbing his chin and appearing to muse wisely, while they sat in a semicircle on the ground.

"Shall the council also desert the village?" he asked, and

they said nothing and only stared into his shadow as it crossed against the fire. "Shall we protect the secret manuscripts? They have become so fragile that they crumble almost at a touch."

All right, I had suspected as much. There were secret manuscripts remaining from the old days. They were full of science, no doubt. Always tyrannic old men try to keep the rest of us ignorant for what they conceive to be our own good. But now the piddling little secrets they had guarded meant nothing to anyone.

Science meant nothing now, either, whatever science was. I had always surmised that science was merely a separate mode of knowledge not so far removed from our customary white magic. The reputation of science had been unjustly blackened when it had been linked to the two earlier failures of civilization that we knew about. But it takes more than a way of knowing things to bring about such momentous collapse. Science, I thought, would be harmless in itself, but perhaps it could be misapplied. You can knock a man's brains out with a lute, but that's not the purpose the lute was designed to fulfill. In my case, I had been gathering wildflowers and comparing their colors, roots, and the shapes of their leaves and petals. Could not our society withstand such a dire enterprise?

Stavros stopped pacing and turned to look into the dark woods. "I do not know," he admitted, "whether we stand in a deep abyss or on the peak of a mountain. I cannot say if there will continue to be a village for us to counsel. Perhaps we no longer are useful to give advice, perhaps our time is past."

He surprised me with that remark. I wouldn't have thought him capable of owning up to the facts. The world had obviously changed even more than I realized.

I rebuked myself. Why had I been so supercilious toward the old men; why did they always bring out that streak of cynical rebellion in me? Just look at them here, harmless elderly uncles and grandfathers, trying not to cling to their old ways, to their specious authority. Think of all those years they had guarded their precious secret manuscripts in which, no doubt, they could not understand a single word. They must have had anxieties, bad dreams I had never guessed at. Now the world had been transformed by the arrival of the Owners and the council was trying to adjust, trying to give up its oppressive habits. Could I not give up my resentment against these stranded anachronisms?

Yes—but not entirely. I would still remember my grievances, but without rancor. My former way of life, and the life of our whole village, now seemed quaint and remote, as delicately remote as a dried flower pressed in a schoolgirl's book of poems. Let me keep my old defiance in mind, then, as a remembrance of days gone by.

I slid out of the undergrowth and climbed back to the road and walked along until I came to an abandoned slaughterhouse. I sat by the slaughterhouse until the late moon rose. I was still different, I thought, from the old men of the council. They were still trying, however falteringly, to make plans for the future. But there was no point in making plans. When our past went away, the future disappeared, too. It was important to keep in mind that the future had died.

The risen moon outlined in the treetops the intricate lodgments of squirrels. Who knows? Tomorrow the trees may consider squirrels their pets and naturally put forth these nests to entice them. Maybe this has already taken place. That's what the future is, the purposes of things becoming apparent too late.

5

I sat by the slaughterhouse till sunrise, then rose refreshed and began walking the road again. I wasn't tired or hungry or even thirsty; I felt I could walk a thousand miles. The air was bright and cool, ringing with bird song. In my youth I had set out like this many times, marching blithely to the river, going to see the morning on the water. I would watch for hours the damselflies over still pools, darting and hovering, drawing angular designs in air. I had been careless in those days.

On the road a long procession approached from behind and I sat on a big white rock to let it go by. A hooded white-robed priest trudged before a coffin borne by six men from my village. A troop of silent mourners shuffled behind the coffin.

I fell in with the procession and plucked Tonio by the sleeve. "Who has died?" I asked.

His eyes were hot and dry. "The widow Larilla," he answered.

I staggered then as from a blow with a cudgel. "That is not possible," I said. "Only last night she was well. She was brushing her hair and singing her little song. It cannot be Larilla who died."

"Nevertheless it is she," he said. "She died of happiness."

I grasped Tonio's arm and pulled him to the ditch. The procession went on by, and he looked at it fretfully. At first I could not speak, the anguish hard in my throat. I flapped my arms and sputtered bits of words.

Tonio eyed me unmoved. "Yes, I know," he said. "You were in love with her, perhaps. But we were all fond of Larilla. And there were others truly in love with her also." He looked away. "Yet we are not sad that she died."

"How—?"

He began to talk with a sudden urgency. "Listen, George, have you ever been happy? Completely happy, I mean, so that there was no other thought or feeling in you but happiness?"

"I don't know."

"Then your answer is no. . . . Larilla was with the Owner. Her happiness was too much for her. She simply spilled out of her body, that's all. That's why we are not weeping." He looked down into the dust. "I think," he said "we are envious of her."

"But she was young and beautiful—"

"And happy," he said. "Now she is young and beautiful and happy forever."

"The Owner is responsible. It's his fault. It's terrible."

"Maybe he told her things we know nothing of," he said. "Perhaps he made love to her. Whatever happened, it was her greatest joy."

"Where is he? I have to talk to him."

His voice became melancholy. "He must have gone away. We looked and couldn't find him."

I began to weep then, but Tonio pressed my hand in his. "No tears," he said. "She was happy."

He drew me into the road and we fell in at the end of the procession, walking along until we came to a grove of bright poplars. We paced on the path through the grove into the homely small graveyard beyond.

They lowered the coffin into the grave and the priest said some words I didn't listen to. Her tombstone was set at the head of the grave, with the epitaph already carved. *Fulfilled,* it said. I noticed that the stone was old and weather-eaten and lichenous; only Larilla's name and the other single word were new.

Then the others went away while Tonio and I remained. I looked down there a long time, but the blank box of yellow pine told me nothing. Finally Tonio led me away. "Let's go back to the village," he said, and we did so. I could not say what I felt as we walked along; I didn't know what to feel.

He led me straight to Larilla's deserted cottage. It was in immaculate order; the village women must have visited in order to clean and straighten. He set me on a stool before the well-scrubbed table and placed a loaf of oat bread before me and poured a cup of water from the pitcher. "Rest," he said. "Eat. Remember. I'll be back in a while to talk with you."

"There are things you haven't told me. Isn't that true?"
"They're not important right now. Just now you'll want
to be alone."
"Yes," I said.
Tonio went away and I sat and stared at the walls for a
long time, still not knowing what to feel. I broke the loaf
of bread and it was full of bright red and yellow sparks.
The sparks flew round and round the room like wasps and
made a musical sound that was the same as Larilla's croon-
ing when she brushed her hair. I became dizzy and steadied
myself by holding on to the edge of the table. Then the
humming swarm of sparks flew up the chimney and disappeared.

The world, you see, was still changing. The Owners had
not finished with it yet. That is why I did not know what
emotions to feel or what signals to observe in the world
about me. A great deal has been revealed to us, but it is
revelation so pure that our minds and senses cannot interpret it. We are not ready.

I decided then, sitting at the table in Larilla's quiet cottage, that I would start again on my journey. I would join
the great army of nameless pilgrims; it was no good sitting
in a room and waiting for the answers to rise from inside
myself. Probably there were no answers in pilgrimage, either, but I was so bewildered and so filled with longing
that I could not stay still. Everything had been revealed to
us, and yet . . .

After revelation, what then?